#5

The Meatless Mayhem Mystery

Books by Maylan Schurch:

Justin Case Adventures:

To order, call 1-800-765-6955.

Visit us at www.reviewandherald.com for information on other

Review and Herald® products.

JUSTIN CASE

#5

The Meatless Mayhem Mystery

MAYLAN SCHURCH

REVIEW AND HERALD® PUBLISHING ASSOCIATION
HAGERSTOWN, MD 21740

This book was
Edited by Randy Fishell
Designed by Tina Ivany
Electronic makeup by Shirley M. Bolivar
Cover art by Thompson Bros., Inc.
Typeset: Cheltenham Book 11/16

PRINTED IN U.S.A.

07 06 05 04 03   5 4 3 2 1

R&H Cataloging Service
Schurch, Maylan Henry, 1950-
      The meatless mayhem mystery.

      I. Title.

                  813.6

ISBN 0-8280-1615-1

Dedication

To Shelley,
>   for 25 happy years
>   and thousands of healthy, heavenly meals.

Thanks

I'm lucky—make that providentially blessed—to have a great editor who's also a good friend. Randy, thanks for the plot nugget you tossed me for this book, and for your gentle editing.

Heather Houck Reseck, fellow member of our Adventist Writers' Association, Shelley and I salute you on the publication of your magnum opus, *Fix-It-Fast Vegetarian Cooking*, in the spring of 2002. Your book does credit not only to your own hard work and attention to detail, but also to the memory of your mother, Fannie Houck, also an AWA member, dedicated writer, and good friend.

Contents

CHAPTER 1

Mystery Girl

As he looked back on it later, Justin Case decided that the adventure started because he was bored.

"Knock-knock," he said to his older brother. It was a Monday in late August, and the two of them were sitting in the morning sunshine on a bench next to the parking lot of the Vitality Resort Hotel near South Dakota's Black Hills.

Actually, Robbie, Justin's older brother, was the only one sitting. Justin was slouching, slouching so far down that his rear end was actually off the bench.

"Knock-knock," he repeated.

"Nobody's home," Robbie growled.

"Come on. Knock-knock."

Robbie didn't take his eyes off the thick travel book he was reading. But his hand flashed out and grasped his brother's slender throat.

"Gock-gock," Justin repeated in a choking voice. "Gon't goo gat, Goggie."

"Lose the knock-knocks then," said Robbie, releasing his grip. "You're 13. You're too old for knock-knock jokes. And yours bug me, because they always sound like you made them up."

Justin massaged his throat and sighed. "If you would

just *listen* to my jokes," he complained, "you would realize that I have raised the knock-knock far beyond the elementary school level. Knock-knock."

Robbie made a sinister fist. "You really want a knock-knock? *I'll* give you a knock-knock."

Justin sighed. "I'm bored."

"What do you think *I* am?"

"But you've got something to read."

Robbie flipped a page. "If you think *The Traveler's Guide to Australia* is a thrill a minute, you're in for a big surprise."

"Nobody's forcing you to read it."

"If I don't read it," Robbie said, "I won't know my way around when I fly over there to start college next week."

"Is your college listed in the book?"

Robbie shrugged. "I don't know. I haven't found it yet."

"Do you think you can find it when you get there?"

There was a slight squeaking sound.

Justin glanced around, his eyes wide. "Are you grinding your teeth?"

"You bet I'm grinding my teeth," Robbie snapped. "Look, if you don't give me some time to myself, I'm going to—"

"OK, OK." Justin slid hastily off the bench and stood up. "When's lunch?"

"I don't know. Go ask Pixie Princess."

"Who?"

"Baby Doll." Robbie jerked his thumb toward the giant glass doors of the hotel's entrance.

"Baby Doll who?" Justin looked around, puzzled. Then he said without thinking, "Knock-knock."

His brother lunged at him.

"Sorry," Justin said, skipping delicately backward a few steps. "I forgot. Is it OK if I do both sides of the knock-knock myself? I just thought of a good one."

"No."

"Knock-knock," Justin said, retreating still farther. "Who's there?" he answered himself. "Baby. Baby who? Baby my cold will be better tomorrow."

"Get out of here," Robbie said flatly.

"Did you get it? 'Baby' is how you say 'maybe' when you have a cold. This guy has a cold, see, and—"

"Move on, little brother."

"And he's hoping that 'maybe' his cold will be gone. But he said 'baby,' because when you have a cold—"

Robbie gently closed *The Traveler's Guide to Australia* and placed it carefully on the bench beside him.

"I'm gone!" Justin yelped, and started up the sidewalk.

The sidewalk led up to the giant glass doors of the four-story Vitality Resort Hotel. The entire Case family—Robbie, Justin, and their mom and dad—were spending part of their vacation in western South Dakota. Mrs. Case was slated to receive the Vitality Vegetarian Foods Volunteer Queen Award, which she had won by being a faithful volunteer cook for Justin's school (and by using a lot of Vitality Vegetarian fake meat).

Lots of other people were headed up the sidewalk too. But as Justin saw who was standing by the door, he paused, then strolled back toward his brother.

"Robbie, who's that girl?"

"You mean Pixie?"

"Yeah. I think I know her," Justin said. "Who is she?"

"If you know her, how come you're asking?"

"I mean, I've seen her before but I don't know her name." Justin fumbled in the beltpack he always wore around his waist and took out something that looked like half a binocular. He focused it.

Robbie took another look too. "Well, *well*," he said in a low voice. "Pink dress, white gloves, golden curls. How old is she, 10? Too young for you."

"She's more like 12 or 13," Justin corrected him. "It's her pink dress that makes her look younger."

"Better put that scope away," his brother warned. "She'll call security on you."

"I know her," Justin repeated. "I've got it—Darla!"

"Darla?"

"Darla," Justin repeated. "Or Darlene. Or Dorothy."

"Those knock-knocks of yours have fried your brain," Robbie said. "I've never heard you babbling girls' names before."

"Doris," Justin said.

"And if you don't give me some peace," growled Robbie, laying his right hand on his *Traveler's Guide* in a solemn vow, "I'm going to walk over to that girl and tell her you want a kiss. Trust me, I will."

Justin, knowing very well that Robbie would carry out his vow, hurried away toward the door. A gentle rumble made him pause and glance back toward the parking lot. A huge silver bus had just turned in from the freeway exit ramp and was moving toward them in a slow, dignified manner.

As he turned back toward the hotel door, a tall, thin, pale boy who looked a little older than Justin hurried by him. The boy had what looked like a digital camera hanging by a strap around his neck. He wore a black T-shirt with the red word "Underside" splashed at an angle across it, and he was chewing earnestly on something.

As Justin moved toward the hotel door he glanced up. The Resort Hotel towered proudly above him, right in the center of the Vitality Vegetarian Foods corporate campus. Over to the right, across a parking lot and a meadow, loomed the ancient Vitality Vegetarian Foods factory itself, with faded silver pipes and tubes coiling on top. The building was made of red brick, and looked picturesque against the deep-blue South Dakota sky.

Suddenly Justin heard a clear, chirpy voice say his last name. "Case?"

He glanced quickly around at the people strolling up the sidewalk. *The girl by the door,* he finally decided, *is the only one with a voice that young.*

But she wasn't looking at him. She was smiling in a hopeful way at a middle-aged woman with a leathery face and a huge purse standing in front of her.

"No," said the woman, "I'm sorry, sweetie." She reached out a hand and patted the girl on her slender shoulder. "Oh, you are *such* a little darling," she sighed, and moved away, staring back over her shoulder.

The girl was now looking at Justin with a smile.

"Welcome to Vitality Vegetarian Foods," she said perkily.

I know that voice, Justin thought to himself. "Uh, hi," he said.

"I hope you enjoy your stay."

He nodded. She was so pretty and her smile was so cute that his face began to feel hot. "Thanks," he said. "I'll try."

"If there's anything we can do to make your stay happier," she continued, as if she was repeating lines in a play, "please let us know."

His face was now flaming. "OK," he mumbled.

"Our tour of the factory is this afternoon at 2:00. If you'd like to come—" She suddenly broke off. "Look," she said in a low voice totally different from her perky one, "can you come with me for a minute? I've got to ask you a question."

His face prickled. "What?"

"Follow me." She switched on her professional smile again, waved to a couple of women who were approaching her with hungry looks in their eyes, and led Justin quickly around the corner of the hotel to a little garden. "Back in here," she said, "out of sight."

As he followed, Justin watched her warily. *The last few months have been interesting,* he thought. *I solved the mystery of a stolen painting at Carnera Bay. I walked through a full-sized Herod's Temple by Arizona moonlight, hoping a hand grenade wouldn't explode under my feet. I chased a crystal dragon in Seattle, and broadcast a youth baseball game in Belize, and almost lost my life on a Kenya safari. But I've never had a cute girl in a pink dress and white gloves try to get me alone.*

"I—uh—know you from somewhere," he said.

She frowned. "Who *doesn't?*" Hurrying over to a huge potted plant, she paused and glanced around, muttered "No Kirkie in sight," and reached beneath the plant with a white-gloved hand. Out came a soda can. Popping the top, she took a couple of gulps. Her eyes locked on Justin's. "I tried to get Kirk to help me, but he said he had to go. Something about a bus."

He began to back away uneasily. "Uh, maybe I'd better—"

She lowered the soda and moved earnestly toward him. "Please don't run off. I'm harmless. I just need your help." She switched on the smile again, and the perk came back into her voice. "I need you to help me find someone. It shouldn't take too long. I'm in trouble."

And it was right here that Justin made his big decision. After all, he was bored.

"What kind of trouble?" he asked.

"*Big* trouble," she said. "I've lost my copy of the guest list somewhere, and I really need to find a lady who's staying here. I thought maybe if you could knock on the second floor doors, I could take the third and fourth floors."

"Well, I guess so," he said. "But can't you just ask at the desk?"

"I don't want them to know that I lost the list."

"Who are you looking for?"

"A Mrs. Case," she replied. "Torah Case."

"Tovah," he corrected her.

Her eyebrows popped up. "You know her?"

"She's my mom."

The girl gave a squeal of relief. "Oh, *cool!*" Into the potted plant went the soda, and out came a bag of cheese curls. "Have some of these," she said, struggling to tear open the bag. "I *hate* these stupid gloves," she snarled. "Nobody wears white gloves any more, but—" She paused, cleared her throat, flashed her smile, and became Miss Perky again. "Sorry."

Justin took the bag from her and opened it. "Why don't you take the gloves off?" he asked. "The cheese curls will get them all orange."

"Yeah, I know." With her left hand she yanked at her right finger ends one at a time. "I need to get to your mom right away."

"She's up in our room," he said. "On fourth. I'll take you there."

"Just a minute." With her ungloved right hand she grabbed a whole fistful of cheese curls and scarfed them down, then reached into the plant again and took another swig of soda. Then she shoved both bag and can back into hiding, brushed off her fingers, and tugged the gloves back on. "Let's go up the rear stairs. What's your name?" she asked as they entered a doorway behind the hotel and began to climb.

"Justin."

"What's your last name? Oh, right. Case." She suddenly giggled. *"Justin Case?* That's really your name?"

"Don't blame me."

"I'll bet you get teased about that."

"Never," said Justin a little sarcastically. "You're the very first one."

"Listen," she said crisply, "you've got it easy compared to me."

"How come?"

She didn't say anything for two more floors. Then suddenly she halted on the stairs and turned to gaze at him. "What kind of mom do you have?"

Justin felt a little dizzy at the way she kept changing the subject. "What do you mean?"

"I mean, like, does she have a sense of humor?"

He nodded. "Sure."

"Does she like to cook? But I guess she does, or she wouldn't have won the Volunteer Queen award. Does she wear an apron when she cooks?"

Justin stared at her. "Not really. How come you want to know all this?"

"Because," she said in a dull, level voice from which all the perk had vanished, "your mom will need to be pretty tough to live through the awards banquet."

"How come?"

"You'll find out," she said.

"Mom's tough."

The girl shook her head. "She's gotta be, like, *really* tough. And another thing, does she pinch you on the cheek?"

Justin blushed. "No."

"Or kiss you on the forehead? Or talk baby talk?"

He shuddered. "Not anymore."

"I've got to see that to believe it," she said cynically. "What floor did you say you're on?"

"Fourth floor. Room 422."

"Here we are," she said, opening a door into a long hallway. "OK, let's meet your mom."

"I already have," Justin said with a smile. "I think you'll like her."

The carpet was soft underneath Justin's sneakers. Glittering chandeliers moved past them overhead as they walked. A blond-haired man brushed quickly past them.

"Don't forget," he said to the girl, turning and walking backward for a moment behind them. "This afternoon. Get it done this afternoon. And I need to talk to you at lunch."

She said nothing, as though she, was pretending not to hear him. After he was gone, she said, "Hi, Mrs. Case," a couple of times to practice her perkiness. "Oh, well," she said to Justin, "pretty soon I'll be a teenager, and there won't be any more of this nonsense."

Justin rapped his knuckles on door 422. "What nonsense?"

She gave him a mocking gaze. "Nonsense like *this.*"

"Like what?"

"Just watch."

The door opened to reveal Tovah Case's alert, watchful gaze. "It's unlocked," she told her son. "You didn't have to knock."

Then she saw the girl.

And to Justin's utter astonishment, his mom's face softened into a sheepish little grin. She reached out both her arms to the girl, and took her by the shoulders.

"Why, it's little Darby," she breathed.

"Darby!" Justin snapped his fingers at the girl. *"That's* your name!"

Then he caught the girl's gaze. Her smile was still perfectly childish and enchanting, but her eyes were like hardened steel.

"You little sweetheart," Mom said softly. She took her right hand off Darby's shoulder and patted the girl's cheek with it.

Mom, Justin thought, *what has gotten into you?*

But the worst was yet to come.

Mom's grin changed to a shy smile. She stopped patting Darby's cheek, extended her index finger, and gently poked the girl on the nose, three times.

"Vitey-vitey-*poo!*" she said.

CHAPTER 2

Busload of Trouble

There was an awkward silence.

"Mom," Justin said in a low voice, *"please!"*

Mom looked at him with glazed eyes, and suddenly the alert look came back to her face. She turned to the girl. "Darby, I'm sorry. Forgive me. Come on in."

Darby came cautiously into the room along with Justin, and closed the door behind her. "That's all right," she said.

"I'll bet this happens to you all the time."

Darby nodded. "All the time."

"But you probably understand why, don't you?"

Darby shrugged.

"I mean," Mom continued, "you practically grew up with my son. How old are you, 11?"

"Twelve."

"That would be right; Jelly Face is 13."

Justin froze. "Mom!" he squawked.

"What?"

"Don't call me Jelly Face!"

Darby's lovely eyes squinted together, and she laughed long and loud. Finally she gasped, "Sorry. It's just"—she took a trembly breath—"it's just so nice to see somebody else get the baby talk besides me."

"Mom," Justin said coldly, "it's been *years* since you called me Jelly Face."

"I know it has," Tovah Case said, red-faced. She gave a muffled giggle. "But seeing Darby brought it all back. Those happy days when my baby boy was 2 years old, bouncing around the room with nothing but his diaper on—"

"Mom!"

"Tell me more," Darby urged between laughs.

"The TV would be on," Mom continued in a dreamy voice, "and the Vitality commercial would start, and oh, Darby, you should have seen him. His eyes would get really huge. And when he saw you on the screen he'd just get the biggest smile all over his fat little face, and he'd bounce up and down and say 'Vah-vah-*poo.*' He liked the 'poo' part best. We just had to make sure he didn't have food in his mouth when he said it."

"That's really funny!" Darby howled.

"Guess what?" Justin said in a voice as cold as a Canadian lake. "I'm starting to remember some of this." He paused. "Vitey-vitey-poo," he continued thoughtfully. "It's sorta familiar. But why?"

Darby took a deep breath, and hiccupped a couple of times. "They drafted me into those commercials when I was 2 years old, and kept me in them till I was 6," she said. "I can't remember much of the earlier years, but I guess they were trying to get me to say 'Vitality Vegetarian Foods.' And anybody in their right mind—except people who make commercials—knows that no 2-year-old on this planet can handle all those syllables. But those commercial makers were pretty sly. *They* knew what would happen. They just started all those cameras rolling and told me to say 'Vitality Vegetarian Foods,' and little innocent me tried to be helpful. And what came out was 'Vitey-vitey-foo.'"

"Poo," Mom corrected her.

The girl shook her head. "Foo."

"Poo," Mom insisted. "Vitey-vitey-*poo!* The poo part was the cutest of all." She reached out both arms. "You just puckered those sweet little lips and—"

"Mom," Justin said in a warning voice. Darby backed warily out of nose-poking range.

"OK, OK," Tovah Case said with a sigh, dropping her arms. "You caught me in my soft spot, that's all. I'm back to reality now. I guess I'd better treat you both like teens. I hope I didn't smudge the makeup on your nose, Darby. It looks all right to me."

"Trust me," the girl said grimly, "I have to go into the bathroom to touch up my nose several times a day during banquet week. And my cheeks. Everybody always pinches my cheeks."

Mom nodded sympathetically. "Maybe if you didn't wear that pink dress, or put your hair up in those darling Shirley Temple curls like you wore in those commercials—"

Darby interrupted. "Do you think I *want* to wear this dress?" she asked in a voice that sounded colder than a Canadian lake. *"Nobody* wears pink these days."

"Why do you do it, then?" Justin asked.

"Great-grandma Cora makes me."

"Aha," Mom said in an understanding voice. "Is she the owner of Vitality?"

Darby nodded. "And she still arranges for a lot of the advertising. Every year they drag me into the studio so I can make new recordings to dub onto the old commercials." She gave a quick shudder. "What's so horrible is that I'm really good at baby talk. What a dead-end talent."

"Do some baby talk for us," Justin said.

She glared at him. "And have me throw up all over your carpet?" she demanded. "Sorry, Mrs. Case. I am just so sick of what they made me do in those days."

"I suppose you are," Mom said. "But it's really nice to meet you. You're almost like a daughter to me—and probably to a million other mothers too. But you said you wanted to see me about something?"

Darby glanced at her watch. "Yes." She became perky and professional again. "Congratulations on winning the Vitality Vegetarian Foods Volunteer Queen award."

Mom shrugged. "It was a big surprise. All of a sudden I got this phone call saying that the principal of our school had sent in my name, and I'd won. I guess I do get involved in a lot of volunteer work, cooking and things like that."

"And," Justin added, "you use a lot of Vitality fake meat."

"Why not?" Mom asked. "It's the best."

"Don't say that too loud," Darby warned her, "or the commercial-maker guys with video cameras will start following you around trying to get you to say 'Vitality Vegetarian Foods.'" She turned to Justin. "And now," she said to him, "I'm going to have to ask you to leave the room."

"Why?"

"Because," she replied, "I need to give your mom her Volunteer Queen orientation."

Mom's eyes got alert. "There's an orientation?"

"Yes."

"And Justin has to leave?"

Darby nodded. "It would be best."

Mom's eyes grew more alert. "Don't I just come up to the front and get the award, and then go back and sit down again?"

"Oh no, Mrs. Case," Darby said gravely. "I'm afraid it's much worse—I mean, I'm afraid there's much more to it than that. Justin, you'd better go."

Justin glanced at Mom, and she nodded. "Go find your dad," she said. "Keep him away, and tell him we might be a little late for lunch."

Outside in the hall, Justin tried to listen at the door for awhile, but he couldn't hear anything except soft murmuring. He'd just turned to walk away from the door when Dad came around a corner.

Robert Case had once been a police detective, but was now a freelance journalist. His schedule had almost kept him away from this trip, but at the last minute he'd been able to come along, which made him happy. He was whistling cheerfully as he approached. But even though he was no longer a police officer, his detecting skills were still sharp, and as he spotted the puzzled look on his son's face his whistling stopped and his eyes narrowed.

"Anything wrong?" he asked.

Justin spread his arms out to block his way. "Don't go into that room."

"Why not?"

"Darby's in there with Mom."

Dad tilted his head curiously. "Darby who?"

"Want to try an experiment?" his son asked.

"Don't have time," Dad said, trying to get past him. "We've got to eat lunch. Darby who?"

"Don't go into that room."

Dad frowned. "Why can't I?" he growled. "And who's Darby?"

"She's my experiment. It's a memory game." Justin switched his voice to a high baby-talk tone. "Vitey-vitey-poo."

"No need to speak Swahili," Dad said impatiently. "We're not in Nairobi anymore." Suddenly his eyes stopped being narrow, then opened wide. "What was that? What did you say?"

"Vitey-vitey-poo."

Dad's jaw dropped for about four seconds. Then his face widened into a strange grin. "Darby Joylander! That little baby in the veggie-food ads! I haven't thought about her in a long time. You say Darby's in our room?"

"Yep, with Mom."

"*Oh,* she was a little doll," Dad said with a cuddly chuckle that Justin never remembered hearing before. "Your mother and I just wanted to reach into that TV screen and pull her out, and raise you two together."

Justin backed warily away. "Don't poke my nose," he said.

Dad blinked. "Why would I poke your nose?"

"You had a nose-poking look in your eye."

"Well hey, let's go say hi to her," his father said cheerfully, trying to move around his son's outspread arms. "I'll say Vitey-vitey-poo to her and see if she remembers."

"Trust me, Dad," Justin said, "she does. And we're not supposed to go in."

"Why not?" His father glanced at his watch and opened his mouth to say something else. But suddenly they heard a loud moan from the other side of the door.

"Noooooooooo . . ."

Dad's eyes grew huge. "It's your mom," he said, fumbling in his pocket for his room key.

"Stay out, Dad. Mom says you gotta stay out."

Dad paused. Then he and Justin crept softly across the carpet and put their ears against the door.

"No, Darby," Mom's faint voice said, "I will not do that. I *cannot* do that."

Darby's voice was too thin for her words to carry through the door, but she seemed to be begging.

"Darby," Mom said again, "don't make me do that."

More muffled begging from Darby.

Dad straightened up. "I guess technically we're eavesdropping," he said softly. "Do you know what's going on?"

"Darby's getting Mom ready for the awards banquet."

"Hmm," Dad said thoughtfully. "How long do you think they'll be?"

"Mom said she might be late for lunch."

"Well, let's go back down to the parking lot. There's something really strange going on down there."

"What?"

"A big bus just got in," Dad said. "A lot of people came out of it holding signs."

"Signs? Are they protesting something?"

Dad nodded.

"What's it about?"

"Let's go down and see."

Back on the main floor, Justin and his dad walked out the lobby door. Several people were standing by their cars or on the sidewalk, watching what was happening in front of the big silver bus. Robbie had gotten up from his park bench and was peering across the parking lot. The thin boy with the black "Underside" T-shirt stood a few feet away, taking pictures with his camera and writing in a small notebook.

"What's up, Rob?" Dad asked.

"Picketers," said his older son.

"Who is it? What are they upset about?"

"I can't tell."

The three of them stared at the 40 or so people who were standing in front of the bus waving large white cardboard signs that had been fastened to new wooden sticks. The signs said things like "VVF LIES!" and "VITA-LIAR, VITA-LIAR, YOUR SOY PATTY IS ON FIRE!" and "STOP DECEIVING THE PUBLIC!" The picketers were shouting the same things the signs said.

"Justin," Dad said, "get out your scope. What does it say on the bottoms of the signs? I can't read it from here."

"B-I-B-I," Justin spelled, after squinting through his scope for a few seconds.

"Bibby?" Robbie asked.

"It must be the initials of some organization," Dad said. "Well, whoever BIBI is, they picked the right time to protest, with all these people coming for the Vitality cooking seminar, and the banquet on Thursday night. Excuse me," he suddenly said to the boy with the "Underside" T-shirt, "do you know anything about this?"

The boy glanced around. He had tiny glasses with square black rims.

"I saw you taking notes," Dad said. "Are you with a school paper?"

The boy shook his head. "Web site."

"Which Web site?"

"The Underside."

"Sorry," Dad said, "but I've never heard of it. Can you tell me anything about these picketers?"

The boy glanced at his notebook. "They're a group called Beef Is Better, Incorporated," he said. "And they're really mad."

"Aha," Dad chuckled.

"They say Vitality Vegetarian Foods is doing false advertising," the boy said. "But I think it's actually because VVF makes veggie meat that tastes so good that it's starting to scare cattle farmers." He peered at the protesters again. "See that short heavy-looking guy standing in the doorway of the bus?"

Before Justin could focus his scope on him the man disappeared inside the bus. "Who's he?" Justin asked.

"Wayne Gimble," the boy replied. "He's BIBI's leader.

He also owns a huge cattle ranch, and Billy's Bigger Burgers fast-food chain. I think he's really worried, especially right now."

"You mean because of the seminar and banquet this week?" Dad asked.

"That too. But Mr. Gimble knows that there's going to be this huge merger of veggie-food companies. VVF is making some sort of deal with two other major producers. One of them's from Southeast Asia. And the more powerful the veggie-food industry gets, the weaker the beef market's going to be."

"Interesting. Well, speaking of food," Dad said, "we'd better get something to eat. Thanks," he said to the boy. "I don't think I caught your name."

"Kirk Levertov."

Justin took a closer look at Kirk, wondering if this was the "Kirkie" Darby had talked about in the garden.

"Thanks, Kirk," Dad said, fishing in his pocket for his own notebook. "Write your Web address right there, and I'll check it out. What's its purpose?"

Kirk grinned. "I'll show you." Once he'd scribbled the Web address, he knelt and clawed at a golfball-sized rock half-buried in the dirt by the sidewalk. Finally he broke it free and held it up.

"The upper side," he said, tapping the top. "Nice and clean and good-looking. The underside," he said, and as he tapped the damp bottom a piece of mud fell off. "Nobody sees the underside until somebody turns the rock over. That's what the Underside Web site does. Everything—politics, business, whatever—has an upper side and an under-side. All most people see is the upper side. Our Web site tries to get underneath all the hype and find the truth."

"Intriguing," Dad murmured. "Which underside are you trying to dig up—Vitality's or BIBI's?"

Kirk held up his notebook. "Both."

"Careful," Dad cautioned him. "Some folks don't like their 'dirt' to be exposed."

Kirk grinned. "I know."

"And now," Dad said to his sons after they'd said good-bye to Kirk and turned their backs on the shouting protesters, "we go and rescue your mother. I wonder what made her wail like that?" He paused, then added, "You know, all this talk about food has made me very, very hungry."

Right then Justin didn't know it, but the crisis that would make the next few days extremely interesting and sometimes a bit dangerous was now only two hours away.

CHAPTER 3

Darby's Dastardly Plan

The Case family had lunch in Mother's Kitchen, a huge restaurant next to the hotel lobby. Mother's Kitchen had frilly curtains on the windows, lots of cozy booths, and a glorious aroma of warm, spicy food.

A red-haired waitress bounded up to their table. She was wearing pigtails and a frilly red-and-white checked apron. "Hi," she said cheerfully. "I'm Mother's little helper. Are you ready to order?"

Justin happened to be looking at his mom right then. Tovah Case stared at the waitress, then slowly closed her eyes.

"Mom," he said, "are you OK?"

Her eyes flicked open in alarm. "What? Me? Oh . . . yes, I'm fine."

Robbie studied her closely. "You look kinda pale," he said.

"Hope you're not coming down with something, hon," Dad murmured.

"Can I get you some antacid?" the waitress asked. "Or aspirin? Mother may have some in her medicine cabinet."

Mom looked her right in the eye. "Tell me one thing," she said firmly. "I know this place is called Mother's

Kitchen, but is there really a 'Mother' back there, or not?"

The waitress grinned and glanced around. "Not really," she said in a low voice. "But they tell us to pretend there is."

Mom nodded. "I thought so." She glanced at the guys. "Go ahead and order," she said faintly. "I don't think I'll have anything."

Robbie and Justin quickly placed their orders. So did Dad, but in a worried voice. "Tove," he said when the waitress had left, "do you want me to take you back to the room?"

She shook her head. Then she glanced at him, a hopeful light in her eye. "Look, Robert," she said, "what do you say we just leave? Get out of here. Tonight."

Dad stared at her. "Leave? How come?"

"Never mind how come," Mom said. "I don't need that Veggie Queen award. They can give it to the runner-up."

"But Mom," Robbie asked, "what about the $1,000 that comes with it?"

Mom gritted her teeth and closed her eyes. "If I actually go through with that banquet nightmare," she said, "it will be only because of that."

"What banquet nightmare?" Dad asked.

"*I'm* all for leaving," Robbie said quickly. "Then maybe I can grab a standby flight to Australia and get there sooner. So let's go."

"What's wrong, Mom?" Justin asked. "What did Darby ask you to do?"

"I refuse to tell you."

By the time the waitress had come back with their soft

drinks, Mom had recovered enough to order mashed pota-
toes and veggie steaks. But no matter how hard her sons or
her husband tried, they couldn't get her to say anything
more. And when the meal was over she rose from the table
looking like a martyr who was getting ready to go walk into
the Roman Coliseum with the lions.

"OK." Dad glanced at his watch as he led the way out of
Mother's Kitchen. "Onward to the factory tour."

"Tour? What tour?" Justin yelped. "I'm not going on any
tour. I'm going upstairs to check for e-mail from Monique
and Rico."

"You are too going on the tour, pal," Dad said firmly.
"Just think what the newspaper headlines would say if the
young son of the new Volunteer Queen sulked in his room
all week. Stock prices would plummet. The entire veggie
meat industry would collapse."

"Mom!" Justin wailed.

"Bite the bullet, Jelly Face," Tovah Case advised him bitterly. "After all, I have to. I can't even count all the teeth-
marks on *my* bullet."

"Jelly Face," Dad repeated thoughtfully. "Ah, it's been a
long time since we called you that. It fit you, though. You
loved your peanut-butter-and-jelly sandwiches. 'Vah-vah-
poo,' you would say happily, and a half-pound slug of
strawberry jam would slam against the opposite wall. Your
pitch had great velocity in those days."

"Dad!"

Justin scowled all the way out the glass doors. He
toyed with the idea of walking over to the protest bus and

asking them for a sign he could wave and holler with. He
kept scowling until he got halfway across the parking lot
toward the huge, funny-looking Vitality Vegetarian Foods
factory. Several people were walking with them, including
a red-haired young woman who had a very pale face and
was wearing a black dress.

At that point he felt a tap on his shoulder. He looked
around. There was a bright little *blink,* and Kirk Levertov
peered around from behind his digital camera.

"Thanks," he said. "Great shot." He fell into step, panting a little, staring hopefully over his tiny black-rimmed
glasses, and holding his small notebook and pencil. He was
still chewing on something.

"Hi," Justin said, smoothing out his scowl.

"Is your name Case?" the other boy said.

"Justin."

"But your last name is Case? Your mom's the VVF
Volunteer Queen?"

Justin nodded.

"Can I interview you?"

Justin blinked. "You mean interview my mom?"

"No, you."

"About what?"

"About how it feels to be the son of the Volunteer
Queen." Kirk poised his pencil over his notebook as he
walked. "How *does* it feel?"

"Fine, I guess," Justin said.

Kirk looked anxious. "Fine? That's all you've got to say?"

"Yeah."

Kirk sighed. "Then how am I going to get 700 words?"

"Seven hundred words for what?"

"For the Underside Web site."

Justin frowned. "You're gonna put my interview on your Web site?"

"Sure. Why not?"

"I'd better think it over. I'm not in too great a mood right now."

"Aha!" A gleam came into Kirk's eye, and his fingers tightened on his pencil. *"Why* aren't you in too great a mood right now?"

Justin glanced at his dad, who was walking about 10 feet ahead. Then he looked up at the bulgy old factory, which was looming above them. "Nothing major. I just didn't want to go on the factory tour, and Dad made me."

"The tour's actually not too bad," Kirk said. "I took it five times last week."

Justin stared. "Five times? Why?"

"Trying to get at the underside—what's really going on under the surface. Listen, Justin," Kirk said, jerking his thumb at the factory, "this place needs to be exposed for what it is. The food they make is so processed that it's a wonder the human body recognizes it at all."

"Really," Justin said politely.

"But the tour itself is cool, because you get to ride on a bunch of small carts hooked together, like a little train."

"You're kidding."

"It's true. *Whoa.*" Kirk's voice suddenly lowered. "An enemy in the camp. There's Wayne Gimble, over to the right.

Those big dark glasses can't fool me. Looks like the owner of Billy's Bigger Burgers is planning to take the tour too."

Once they'd entered a large room with about 20 other people, they were met by the same blond-haired man Justin had seen in the fourth-floor hall, the one who'd told Darby he needed to talk to her at lunch and to make sure she got something finished that afternoon.

"Ladies and gentlemen," the man said, "the tour is about to begin." He looked like he was about Dad's age, and was wearing a headset with a little black microphone that curled around in front of his mouth. The sound of his voice echoed from tiny loudspeakers on a little four-car train. Each of the train's cars held six people, and once everyone was on, the man sat down in the driver's seat. With a faint electric hum and a shrill *beep-beep* the train began to move.

"Welcome to the Vitality Vegetarian Foods Heritage Tour," said the man. "My name is Donald Joylander, and I'll be your host. I'm part of the VVF family in more ways than one. My grandmother, Cora Joylander, is chairman of the Vitality board—she's probably in the building somewhere even as we speak."

Kirk, who had crowded in beside Justin, whispered, "She's a tough old woman. I tried to interview her for Underside once, and she got really mad."

"Did you each get your information packet?" Mr. Joylander asked, holding up a humungous brown paper bag with handles on top and "Vitality Vegetarian Foods" written on the side. "Inside you'll find lots of brochures and recipes, and even a few samples of VVF jerky. By the way," he continued, "I hope you enjoy your method of transportation. You're now riding on the Energy Express. Taking this little train is so much easier than walking through the factory—and it helps keep outside dust to a minimum so we can have a more sanitary place to prepare all those tasty meat substitutes our great land is learning to love. I'm just going to circle around here in the Heritage Room for a minute and let you look at the pictures on the walls."

Justin sighed, and slumped in his seat. He found the Heritage Room big-time boring. Its walls were covered with old black-and-white photos. Some of them showed the factory, which looked like it had been added on to over the years, which was probably what gave it its bulgy look.

Kirk elbowed him. "Darb hates this room," he whispered. "You know Darb?"

"Darby Joylander?" Justin whispered back. "How come she hates it?"

"Look." The other boy waved his arm toward a wall Justin hadn't seen yet.

The wall was totally filled with pictures of Darby in her younger years—Darby in diapers, Darby in pajamas, Darby making a snowman, Darby on Santa's lap, Darby on horseback, Darby putting on her mother's lipstick, Darby looking sweetly into the camera making an "oo" with her lips.

"Did you know her dad and mom are divorced?" Kirk whispered. "She wanted to go spend time with her mom this summer, but Great-grandma Cora kept her here working on commercials."

The little train turned down a long hallway. "Here are the corporate offices," said Darby's dad. "Mine is coming up on your left. I'm a vice president, and one of my duties is director of public relations."

Kirk suddenly elbowed Justin excitedly. "Look!" he whispered. "Darb's in there. See her through the glass window in that door? Mr. J," he called out, "mind if Justin and I jump off here?"

The man paused slightly, then said "OK, Kirk," and brought the train to a halt.

Dad turned around, a puzzled look on his face.

"Just for a few minutes, Mr. Case," Kirk begged him. "The train comes through here again in half an hour. We'll stay close by."

Dad shrugged and nodded, and the two boys got off.

"Your dad seems like a nice guy," Kirk said as the little train hummed away. "What does he do?"

"He used to be a police detective. But now he's a journalist."

Kirk raised his eyebrows, impressed. "Cool." He paused outside the office door. "It's our duty to go bother Darb," he said. "She hates taping."

"Taping?"

"Well, I guess it's not really tape—it's digital. But she's doing narration for a PowerPoint documentary for Thursday night's banquet. It's sort of a look back on all the commercials she's ever done."

"Maybe we'd better not bug her," Justin said, and told his new friend about seeing Darby's dad in the hotel hallway, and what he'd said to her.

"Trust me," Kirk said earnestly. "I know her really well. She goes to the same school I do. She gets sick of hanging around adults all the time, having to be cute to them. She needs us."

Through the window in the door they could see the back of Darby's golden head. She was wearing a headset with a microphone, and was seated facing a computer screen, her right hand on a mouse and her left hand holding a piece of paper. Kirk turned the doorknob noiselessly and they entered.

"—and here I am at age 5," Darby was saying in a child-like voice. "Papa and Mama took me to Billy's Bigger Burgers for the very first time!" Her right hand moved the mouse and clicked it. "And here I am, in the booth, just chewing away at this really huge chunk of dead cow, loving every minute of it. Mama says I cried when they wouldn't let me have a second burger. I guess I really loved that good old bloody red meat."

Justin and Kirk stared at each other, eyes wide.

"But then, later in the year," Darby chirped, clicking the mouse again, "Papa brought home some sliced ham. And it was then that I discovered that there was a meat I loved even more than hamburger and lobster."

Suddenly Kirk grinned. "She's faking," he whispered. "She knows we're here. Hi, Darb," he said loudly. "Let's hear some more about your first ham sandwich."

But neither boy was prepared for how Darby reacted. She screamed loudly, whipped off the headset, leaped to her feet and turned. Justin saw that beneath her little-girl rosy-cheeks makeup her face was white.

"Where did—how did—" she sputtered.

"You're good, Darb. Really good. Eyes in the back of your head. How did you spot us coming?"

"Kirkie," she gasped. "What rock did you slither out from under?" Her eyes flicked to Justin. "Hi," she said, and he noticed she didn't look as perky as before.

"We saw you in here," Kirk said, "and we figured it was our duty to bug you. Hey, what's this?" he said with great interest, staring at the screen.

She grabbed the mouse and began clicking wildly, but couldn't hit the right spot, and the picture stayed frozen on the monitor. It was a picture of her, maybe 5 years old, all smiles and golden curls, seated at a table where a half-eaten roast pig was spread out on a platter.

"Darb," said Kirk in a shocked voice, "what's with you? What's going on here?" He cleared his throat and reached for the mouse. "This isn't your PowerPoint show for the banquet. At least, I *hope* it isn't."

"Give me that mouse," she snapped.

"Maybe I should go back to the tour," Justin suggested tactfully.

"I think you should stay," Kirk said. "Darb, what's the problem?"

"You both should just leave," she said in a wobbly voice.

"Are you in trouble?"

"You're in trouble. Or you will be when I call security." Suddenly she burst into tears.

Kirk and Justin looked at each other again, this time uneasily. Their glances seemed to say, *What do you do with a crying girl?* Finally Kirk cleared his throat.

"Darb," he said quietly, "just tell us about it. What's wrong?"

"You wouldn't understand!"

Kirk reached into his pocket and pulled out a clear plastic baggie filled with what looked like shiny little green beans about the size of M&Ms. "Have some raw soybeans, Darb," he said. "They'll calm you down."

She cupped her hand and slowly held it out.

"Good," he said gently, and began to tip the bag.

But once her hand was full of soybeans, she flung them energetically across the room. They rattled against the wall and plopped onto the carpet.

Kirk's jaw dropped. "I'm going to go get your dad," he said. "You need to go home."

She reached out and grabbed him by his Underside T-shirt. "You stay right here. Nobody's going for Papa. Right?" She glared at Justin. "That goes for you too."

"Sure," said Justin quickly.

"And you two guys are going to have to promise me something else," she said in a level voice. "You did not see these pictures, OK?"

"But what *are* they?" Kirk asked, trying to pry her fingers off his shirt. "They can't be real. Your mom and dad are vegetarians. They never took you to a burger place in your life. You must have faked those photos."

She sniffed, and grinned a little grin through her tears. "Of course I faked the photos." With her free hand, she

rolled the mouse and clicked it, slower this time, and the pig photo vanished.

"Why?" Kirk had now managed to get two of her fingers loose.

But she tightened her grip. "Because," she said, *"this* is the PowerPoint documentary that's going to flash up on the screen at Thursday night's Vitality Awards Banquet."

CHAPTER 4

Poem of Doom

In the silence that followed Darby's remark, Justin and Kirk glanced at each other. Finally Justin timidly cleared his throat.

"You know," he said to the girl, "if somebody looks through the window in that door, it's going to seem kind of funny the way you're hanging onto Kirk by his shirt."

She heaved a huge sigh, then said, "Yeah, I suppose so," and released the T-shirt. "But look," she said, "you guys just don't know what all I've been through."

"You've told me some of it," Kirk said. "Your great-grandma forced you to stay here this summer dubbing commercials and doing publicity stuff when you wanted to be with your mom."

"True, but that's not all. Papa talked to me at lunch today."

"About what?"

She stared at him stonily. "I'm not going to tell you if you're going to splash it all over your web site."

Kirk sighed. "OK, even though I still need 700 words. The picture on the screen caught his eye again and he gave it a worried look. "Darb, that PowerPoint thing. You're not really going to show it at the banquet, are you?"

"I might."

"Where's the real one, the documentary about all your commercials? Haven't you done anything on that?"

She grinned again, this time shamefacedly. "That's been done for weeks. I kept pretending to Papa that it wasn't, and he keeps hassling me to get over here and finish it. So I come over here and work on the fake one."

"So what did you find out at lunch?" Kirk asked.

Her face turned stony again. "None of this goes on the Web site, understand? At least not until after Thursday night."

"OK, I promise."

Her eyes burned with fury. "It turns out that Great-grandma Cora has plotted another terrorist act. I thought I was done with all of the 'smile-for-the-camera-Darby' stuff. Not a chance. I should have known better."

"She wants you to do more commercials," Kirk guessed.

"You've got it."

"But you can't be Baby Darby forever."

"Oh, this isn't Baby Darby," she said bitterly. "Oh, no. This is *Teenage* Darby. 'Little Darby's growing up,'" she said in a fake announcer's voice, "'and you know why? Because every day she packs her little tummy with Vitality Vegetarian Food.'"

"Hey, look," Kirk said, "it's a job. They pay you, don't they?"

"Of *course* they pay me," she said impatiently. "Money's not the thing. I've got more money than I know what to do with. But I wanted to go stay with Mama for a while. And here all of a sudden I've got to learn another set of scripts and act cute again. And now instead of all those adoring mothers pinching my cheeks, it'll be four million boys writing to me. And wanting me to go steady with them." She paused, then added, "And maybe stalking me."

"You don't like boys?" he asked.

"Not four million of them," Darby replied. Suddenly a sly smile crossed her face. "Hey, Kirk, give me another soybean. Make that two, one for each of your nostrils."

"You threw them all away."

"Sorry about that."

"It's OK. But you really do need to eat more soybeans," Kirk said earnestly. "Soybeans stabilize your emotions."

"And," she said, looking him up and down, "they make *you* scrawny and pale."

"Soybeans are *good* for you," he repeated firmly. "Not when they're all splattered over the floor, of course."

She sighed. "I'll clean them up."

"And you'd better delete that fake PowerPoint show."

She shook her head. "I'm *not* going to delete it. I worked hard on it. It's got lots of good stuff. I even came up with a scene where Dad takes me on my first deer-hunting trip. And I tell everybody that Vitality fake ham has real ham fat in it. And I'm going to do one where Mom teaches me how to cook opossum."

"Well at least don't leave it on the hard drive."

"I'm not *stupid*, Kirkie. It's on this CD and nowhere else." She rattled a few computer keys and then poked at a button on the computer tower. When a tray slid out she removed the shiny silver disk and put it into a CD jewel case.

Justin saw that the case had "DARBY—PRIVATE" written on it in black marker.

"Better keep it out of sight," Kirk urged her.

"I *will*," she snapped, sliding the case and the script she'd been reading between the pages of a teen magazine thrust into a side pocket of her backpack. "Keep an eye on this for me—I'll be right back. No, on second thought I'm taking it with me," she said with a suspicious glance at Kirk. "I don't want you putting it back in the computer and punching through it. Might be too tempting for your Earthworm Web site."

"Underside," he corrected.

"Whatever," Darby responded, picking up her backpack and heading for the door.

"I suppose," Justin said once she'd gone, "we could gather up these soybeans for her."

Together they knelt on the floor and began collecting the beans. Kirk muttered, "Did you see the cover of that teen magazine she had in her pack?"

"No."

"It was a whole issue on diet and weight loss. That's the last thing Darb needs."

"She looks thin already," Justin agreed.

"Know how she keeps herself that way? She's a vegetarian, which is great, but she also scarfs down a lot of fatty snack foods, and then she goes into the bathroom and barfs a lot of it back up."

A chill went down Justin's back. "Does she have ane— ana—" He paused, trying to remember the word.

"Anorexia? If she doesn't, it sure seems like she's getting close." Kirk landed flat on his stomach and wriggled his arm under Mr. Joylander's huge desk. "You know, as soon as she mentioned that Teenage Darby ad campaign, I got this funny feeling. You know how TV stars have to keep themselves really thin because TV makes you look fatter than you are?"

"Oh-oh," Justin said. "You mean Darby might starve herself even more?"

Kirk sneezed from a bit of dust he'd stirred up, then sat up again clutching a handful of soybeans. "If they can get her to agree to the commercials, she probably will. I wish she'd just listen to common sense. She doesn't have to starve herself to look great. All she's got to do is eat right."

"But raw soybeans?" Justin said doubtfully.

"Not *only* raw soybeans," Kirk insisted. "Just raw stuff in general. Raw apples, raw nuts, raw carrots, raw everything."

"Why raw?"

"Do you believe in the Bible?"

Justin blinked. "Sure."

"Good." Kirk crawled off in another direction, hunting more beans. "Do you remember what Adam and Eve ate in the Garden of Eden?"

"The Bible doesn't say, does it?"

"Oh yes it does. In the last few verses of Genesis 1. Fruits, nuts, grains, that kind of thing. And do you think they had fire to cook with in Eden?"

"I never thought about it," Justin replied.

"Well *think* about it," Kirk urged him. "Perfect world,

right? No fire needed, right? No fire, no boiling water. Everything raw."

"Could be," Justin said cautiously.

"So if God created us," Kirk continued, "and I believe He did, then He gave Adam and Eve the best possible diet. So," he grinned, holding out a palm filled with several dusty beans, "have a soybean. That's pretty much all I eat these days."

"Maybe next time," Justin replied.

Darby still hadn't returned by the time they heard the *beep-beep* of the returning Energy Express down a distant hallway. They hurried through the office door and started walking toward the Heritage Room.

"Where's the restroom?" Justin asked.

Kirk pointed. "Go through the Heritage Room and down the hall beyond," he said.

Justin hurried on ahead. Darby's photos smiled down at him, and he passed through the far door at the same time the Energy Express was entering the room at the other side. The restrooms were on the left, both men's and women's. As he emerged from the men's restroom, Darby was coming out of the women's restroom with her backpack. She looked very pale.

"Hi," he said.

"Hi," she replied.

"We cleaned up the soybeans."

She giggled wearily. "Sorry you had to get mixed up in all that messy stuff. I didn't mean to be snotty or anything. It was just such a shock to get the word from Papa that I'm still Darby the Advertising Slave."

"Can't you refuse?"

"I could," she said, "but that would put Papa in a bad spot. He's not on very good terms with Great-grandma Cora. She's always threatening to put him back in sales. He's good at sales, but he hates it. Great-grandma Cora's got her iron grip on everybody, and we pretty much have to do what she says." She smiled bravely at Justin. "Just forget about all of this. I don't want to spoil everything for you. After all, your mom won the award, and you ought to be happy, right?"

They walked together back to the Heritage Room. Then Darby darted past the tourists toward her dad's office, and Justin made his way to where his family was standing. Both Robert Cases, senior and junior, were gazing up at the Baby Darby photos.

"I suppose she's spoiled rotten by now," Robbie said.

"Not really," Justin told him.

"How do *you* know?"

"I've met her."

Robbie stared. "You have?"

"That was her standing by the hotel door this morning."

Dad sighed. *"I'd* like to meet that little gal," he said.

"Let's get out of here," Tovah Case said tersely.

* * *

Justin was the first one into room 422, and that meant that he was the first to see the large white paper bag on the recently made bed.

"Whose is this?" he asked.

The rest of the family made vague "I don't know" and "The maid must have left it" noises, so he peeked in the top.

"Hey, it's an apron," he said, pulling it out. "A white frilly one. And here's a big red rolling pin, and a spatula, and a—"

Suddenly the bag was snatched out of his hands.

"Mom!" he protested, "let me see!"

"I'll take charge of this," Mom said grimly.

"What is it?" Dad asked.

She stared at him, jaw tight, clutching the bag tightly to her. "This," she said, "is my costume for banquet night."

Robbie glance over with interest. "Costume? You've got to wear a costume?"

"Put it on, Mom," Justin suggested.

"Not on your life," she said shortly.

Justin noticed a piece of paper on the floor, and remembered seeing it fall as Mom grabbed for the bag. He casually picked it up and turned his back, scanning it. Then he wandered over to the furthest corner of the room, turned, and began to read aloud in a sweet feminine voice:

Chorus:
I'm a Vivacious VVF Cook!
I love to cook! I don't need a book!
I'm queen of the kitchen, and proudly reign
With greatest joy o'er my domain.

Dad stared. "You've got to be kidding."

Mom lunged for her son, but Justin whirled around, evading his mother's grasp. He continued reading:

Verse 1:
My happy hubby enjoys my meals,
And many a grateful kiss he steals!
Here's my secret—I won't keep mum—
The way to his heart is through his tum.
         (Chorus)

"It says to do the chorus again," Justin said apologetically, and did so. Then, in spite of Mom's dire threats, he launched into the next verse:

Verse 2:
Gone from my larder are fleshy foods
Beef and pork and similar goods!
Hubby blesses the happy day
I learned to cook the Vitality way!
         (Chorus again)

"I'm sorry, but it says I've got to read the chorus again," Justin said.

"Wait a minute," Robbie said, as though very confused. "What's a 'hubby'?"

"I'm not sure," Justin replied.

"I'll eat you guys alive," Mom said, making another attempt to extract the document from Justin's grasp.

"But if you did that," Justin reminded her, "you

wouldn't be eating the Vitality *Vegetarian* way."

"What's a 'hubby'?" Robbie asked again in a pathetic voice.

"Tell you what," Justin said tactfully, "I'll just skip the chorus and go on to the final verse."

Verse 3:
I'll never go back to my former cuisine!
There are better ways to get my protein!
With hubby so happy, my life is serene!
I'm glad to be this year's Vitality Queen!

"I still want to know what a hubby is," Robbie complained.

Robert Case Senior couldn't answer that question, mainly because he was lying on his back on the floor, kicking the carpet with his heels and choking with laughter. "With hubby so happy, my life is serene!" he hooted.

"And many a grateful kiss he steals," Robbie reminded him.

"And many a grateful kiss he steals," Dad repeated between gasps.

"Maybe I should read the whole thing again," Justin offered.

At this, Mom summoned some superhuman energy and leaped upon Justin. Wrenching the paper from his grasp, she quickly folded it.

"Mom," Robbie said, "did you write that? What amazing poetry! What a lyrical masterpiece!"

"Of course I didn't write it," she snapped. "And if you don't back off this very instant, I'll start telling stories about you. And I know some good ones."

"My favorite part," Justin said, "is the line 'I'm a Vivacious VVF Cook.'"

"And that," Mom said flatly, "is enough out of *you.*"

Everybody except Mom roared with laughter. They laughed so loudly that they didn't hear the first ring of the telephone. But Justin heard the second, and he ran to answer it.

"Hello?"

"Justin, is that you?" It was a girl's voice, very small and afraid.

"Darby?"

"Justin, you know that CD I made? It's gone."

CHAPTER 5

Missing CD

Robbie and Dad were still howling with laughter and trying to remember bits and pieces of the poem.

Justin jammed a palm against his free ear to shut out the noise. "What was that, Darby? You say your CD's gone?"

"Yes! Can you please come help me look for it?"

"Probably, but I need to ask first. Hang on." He put a hand over the mouthpiece. "Dad, Darby wants me to come back over to the factory for a little bit."

Dad took a deep, trembly breath. "Oh, that was fun," he said. "I haven't laughed so hard in all my—what's that, Jelly Face?"

"The factory. Darby wants me to come over for a bit. She's lost something, and she wants me to help her look for it."

Dad glanced at his watch. "OK. Be back at suppertime. Six o'clock—got that? And invite Darby up to the room sometime. I'd like to meet her."

When Justin got back to the Heritage Room, all he saw was a group of about 15 women gazing at Darby's pictures and chatting about them. As he wandered across toward the corporate hallway, Darby suddenly poked her head out of her dad's office and beckoned to him.

"Sorry I couldn't be out front," she said after he'd come in and she'd closed the door. "But those women would have gotten hold of me. Thanks for coming over."

"No problem."

She sighed. "I hope I wasn't interrupting something when I called. From the background noise, it sounded like you were all having a good time."

Justin grinned. "Yeah. Somebody had dropped off Mom's costume for the banquet, and I got hold of the 'Vivacious VVF Cook' poem." He suddenly sobered. "You didn't write that, did you?"

She rolled her eyes. "No way. Great-grandma Cora wrote it—40 years ago. And it's not a poem, it's a song."

"A *song?*"

She nodded solemnly. "And your mother is going to have to sing it."

Justin's jaw dropped.

"And during the chorus she has to wave the rolling pin in time to the music so the audience can sing along."

Justin stared into space, trying to picture his mom in a frilly white apron cheerfully waving a bright red rolling pin at a whole roomful of people, trying to get them to sing along with her. Suddenly he shook his head as if he was waking from a weird dream.

"Your CD," he said. "You can't find it?"

Her eyes were wide with fear. "I've looked for it again and again. I don't dare go out to the Heritage Room with all those cheek-pinchers and shoulder-patters. I just can't take that right now. Would you look around out there for me? I'll go through this office again."

"Did you check out the women's restroom?"

She nodded. "I went around by a back way. It's not there."

"OK," Justin said, heading for the door. "I'll come back here when I'm done."

He spent 15 minutes in the Heritage Room flipping through brochures and pretending to look at the photos on the walls, but really hunting for any place where the CD might have dropped. He even stared at the women's purses when he thought nobody was looking, to see if there were any square-cornered bulges.

When he got back to Mr. Joylander's office, Darby was scrunched up in a huge armchair, paler than ever.

"Sorry," he said, "not a sign of it."

Darby gulped mournfully. "This is bad news."

"I know you had it with you when you left Kirk and me in the office."

"I know, in my magazine in the backpack. I went right to the restroom and then saw you coming out of the men's restroom. We walked back to the Heritage Room together and you split off to join your family, and I came back here."

"When did you notice it was gone?"

She hugged her own shoulders and shivered. "I checked my e-mail and surfed the Internet for a while," she said, glancing at the computer. "Then I decided to work on the CD some more. I looked in the magazine, and the CD wasn't there. Case and everything—it was gone." She shivered again. "That's bad news. Really bad news."

"You looked in the rest of your backpack?"

She nodded. "Of course, again and again."

"The CD case said 'DARBY—PRIVATE' on it," he reminded her. "Maybe somebody's got it and they'll bring it back to you later tonight or tomorrow. Anyway, nobody *knew* you were making that fake documentary, did they?"

The phone rang. Darby stared at it in annoyance until it stopped. Then it rang again. "Let's get out of here," she said.

"The women are still in the Heritage Room," he warned her.

"I don't mean through there," she said. "Let's go out through the factory."

Together they hurried down one hall, then another, and finally through a swinging door into a large room with huge steel vats and a steamy smell. From there Darby led the way down a dark hallway filled with hissing pumps and machines, and out the other end to a huge, sunlit loading dock.

"Over here," she said, leading Justin to where four motor scooters were parked. "You take the black one." She slid onto the seat of the red one beside it, and flicked a switch.

He frowned doubtfully. "Are you sure we're supposed to use these?"

"They're for the supervisors to get around the factory quickly," she said. "We've got a big plant, but they always let me ride them if I bring them back."

"But I never drove one of these before."

"You ride bikes, right?"

"Sure."

"This is just a bike with an electric motor. It doesn't go too fast. Here," she said as she flicked a switch in front of him. "Now it's on. Just put it in gear and turn the handle. Slow," she said, as his rear tire squeaked and he lunged ahead.

Somehow Justin jerked the machine to a halt and Darby gave him some more instructions, including how to stop. After a few cautious circles around the loading dock platform Justin said, "Where are we going?"

"Back to the hotel."

"Wait a minute," he said. "How are we going to get off the dock?"

She pointed to one end of the dock. "That ramp over there."

"Whoa. That's steep."

"It's easy," she said. "Like this." With a loud hum she scooted across the dock and with a thump and a rattle disappeared rapidly over its edge. "Nothing to it!" she called, circling into view below.

Justin cautiously steered the scooter to the edge of the ramp and rolled down it, lurching and wobbling all the way, keeping a firm grip on the brakes.

"Now," Darby said, rolling up beside him, "let's stop right here for a minute. There's something we have to figure out."

They glanced thoughtfully at each other.

"Kirk," Justin guessed.

"Yep," she replied. "Kirkie's either a friend or a suspect."

"You know him better than I do," Justin said, "but back there in your dad's office he *seemed* like he was on your side. I mean, he even offered you some soybeans to calm you down."

She looked sideways at him from under her beautiful lashes. "Is that true?"

"Is what true?"

"Can raw soybeans really calm you down?"

He shrugged. "My mom knows a lot about health, and I've never heard her say anything about soybeans calming people down, raw or not."

"I know that Vitality uses soybeans in just about every-thing they make," she said. "But Kirkie's really into raw. Raw this, raw that. Raw, raw, raw, that's all you hear."

"Like in a cheerleading squad," Justin said.

She glanced at him. "What?"

"You know. That's what cheerleaders yell. 'Rah, rah, rah!'"

"Oh, I get it." She wrinkled her nose. "You never told me you were a stand-up comedian."

"I'm not. I just like jokes."

"Too bad it wasn't you that won the Volunteer Queen Award."

Justin raised his eyebrows. "Besides my not being a girl," he inquired, "why do you say that?"

"It sounds like you love to perform corny comedy," she said. "And your poor mom doesn't."

Justin burst into laughter. "You should have seen her," he chuckled. "I was reading that poem out loud, all about hubby being happy and stealing grateful kisses and every-thing. Dad was rolling on the floor laughing."

She frowned. *"Men.* You're all alike. Your poor mother."

"It wasn't *our* fault," he insisted. "It was thinking about her having to wear that funny apron and wave that bright. red rolling pin and do that looney poem. We didn't know it was a song. A song is gonna be even more fun to watch. What else is she going to have to do at the banquet?"

"I'm not telling you," Darby said firmly. "You're just going to have to wait and see. But let's cut the chatter and decide about Kirkie."

"He seemed OK to me," Justin said hesitantly.

"Yeah, I'm pretty sure Kirkie's cool," she agreed. "Let's go find him. I know where he is. I was looking out through Papa's window just before you got there, and I saw Soybean Superhero out beside the demonstrator's bus. He had this big wad of brochures under his arm."

Justin grinned. "He needs 700 words for his Web site article. But are you really sure that your CD wouldn't be too big a temptation for him?"

Darby shook her head. "He and I have known each other for a long time." Her scooter began to move. "And anyway," she called back over her shoulder, "if he had the CD and wanted to use it, he wouldn't be wasting time collecting brochures from protesters. He and Wally would be hunched over a computer monitor dumping it onto their Web site."

Justin hastily lurched his scooter into motion and started to follow. "Who's Wally?"

"The Webmaster for Underside," she shouted back. "By the way, if Wally gets that CD, we're dead. Wally has no conscience."

Together they hummed around the far end of the

Vitality factory. Justin noticed how huge it really was, with wing after wing added on, out in back where you couldn't see them from the front.

Eventually they rounded the final corner and aimed their scooters for the main parking lot. The huge silver bus was still there, with a lot of people standing around watching the protesters. Sure enough, Kirk was there too, brochures still under his arm, flashing away with his camera and talking to Wayne Gimble.

"Pull up for a minute," Darby said, slowing down so she was side-by-side with Justin. "We've got to be quick. You scoot in there and tell Kirkie to ride behind you and then follow me. There are too many cheek-pinchers nearby. If they spot me in this pinky-winky dress, we'll never get out of there alive. *Go.*"

Off she sped toward the hotel. Halfway there she stopped to wait. Near the hotel entrance a motherly woman in the crowd tapped another motherly woman on the arm, and pointed at the distant Darby. Both then tapped other motherly women on the arms.

"Excuse me, excuse me," Justin said again and again as he nosed the lurching scooter through the crowd near the bus. "Excuse me, please."

Finally he reached Kirk's side, where Wayne Gimble was talking to him earnestly in a high, piercing voice.

"What I can't understand," Wayne said, "is that if meat is so bad for people, how come Vitality makes products that *pretend* to be meat? Why don't they just make something else? But no—it's fake hamburger, fake steaks, fake

bacon, fake chicken, fake turkey, fake sausage. Every new fake meat they make is a lie. It's pretending to be something it isn't? Am I right?"

Kirk didn't answer, but wrote busily in his notebook.

"And the more they make their fake meat taste like the original, the more they're proving my point."

"What is your point?" Kirk asked, writing fast.

"Meat is what people really need," Wayne Gimble insisted. "And what I say to the people of this nation, and the people browsing your Web site, is this: Why buy the fake stuff when you can go to a Billy's Bigger Burgers and have the real thing? Why buy the lie? Answer me that!"

Before Kirk could answer him, Justin cleared his throat. "Uh, Kirk, we need you to come right now."

Kirk finished writing a sentence, put a period on it, and glanced around. "Hi, Justin. What's up?"

"Bad news."

Mr. Gimble looked very interested. "Bad news? What's wrong?"

CHAPTER 6

Who's Calling?

"Just—some bad news," Justin repeated cautiously. The scooter lurched a little. "Sorry," he told Kirk. "We need you right now. Hop on."

Now it was Kirk's turn to be cautious. "Do you know how to drive that thing?"

"Sure," Justin said, lurching again. "We really need you right now."

"Well, stop jerking like that and I'll trust you more." Kirk climbed on quickly. "Thanks for your time, Mr. Gimble," he said to the man. "Can we pick this up where we left off later?"

"Of course," Wayne Gimble said grandly. "Anytime. And when did you say your article would be on the Web site?"

"Tomorrow," Kirk said.

The scooter lunged forward. Justin clung tightly to the handlebars, and Kirk clung tightly to Justin.

"What's up?" Kirk said into Justin's ear. "And slow down. I'm losing brochures."

The scooter went even faster. "Sorry," Justin gulped. "I turned the handle the wrong—*yeeowtchhh!*" The scooter ran over something hard and rose sharply in the air.

"That was part of the curb!" Kirk said loudly into Justin's other ear after they had thumped to earth again, miraculously still on two wheels, "Slow *down,* would you? Better yet, let me drive."

"No, no, I'm getting the hang of it," Justin said in a confident voice.

"That *cat!*" yelped Kirk. "Watch out for—"

"Missed him," Justin said with relief.

Behind him, Kirk shuddered. "That cat's left whisker is only half as long as it used to be. Slow *down!*"

"I'm going to get Dad to buy me one of these," Justin said, swooping sharply to the right.

"Tell me sometime which state you're from," Kirk begged, "so I can take my vacation in the opposite direction. Where," he asked in a pleading voice, "is the Army National Guard when we need it?"

Somehow—and neither Justin nor Kirk knew exactly how—they ended up safely behind Darby's scooter. They lurched along after her to the rear of the huge Vitality Resort hotel, and came to a stop alongside a high thick hedge. The girl hopped off, hurried to a wooden door situated amid the hedge, and punched a number into a security keypad. Turning the knob, she pushed the door open and beckoned to them.

"Kirkie, drive my scooter in here. Justin, bring yours too."

As Justin lurched his scooter through the door, he discovered that they were inside a combination basketball and tennis court. A door at the far end led directly into the hotel.

"We're safe here," Darby said, closing and locking the door. "This is the Joylanders' private outdoor gym," she told Justin. "I'll be right back after I change into jeans." She darted through the far door and disappeared.

"Ouch," Kirk said to Justin. He was shuffling the brochures he still had left into a neat stack. "When did you learn to drive scooters?"

"About 10 minutes ago."

Kirk nodded. "I figured so. Well, what's the bad news?"

"Uh, I think we need to wait for Darby to get back."

Kirk snorted. "This had better be important. I was getting a lot of good stuff out of Mr. Gimble." He fished in his pocket, pulled out an empty baggie, and scowled at it. "I'm starving," he grumbled. "If Darb wouldn't have wallpapered her dad's office with my soybeans I'd have something to eat right now."

Darby was back in a couple of minutes, in jeans and T-shirt. She grabbed a basketball from a corner of the court. "Kirkie! Justin and I will take you on! Kirkie's tall," she explained to Justin, "and he thinks he's the best basketball player in the county."

"No I don't," Kirk said in an annoyed voice, but he leaped to join them. And for a few minutes the three of them battled it out. Once when Darby dashed past him, Justin caught the aroma of cheese curls. *She must have a stash in her apartment,* he thought.

Then he noticed that Kirk had slowed down and was trying to get his breath.

"Kirk," Darby shouted, "what's the matter?"

"I'm starving," he snapped. "And it's all because you tossed my lunch all over your dad's office."

"You need more than just raw soybeans to keep your strength up," she told him. "Why didn't you *say* you were hungry? I could have brought down a bag of cheese curls. Or a Vitality hot dog. Forget the raw soybeans."

Kirk gathered his strength and lunged for the ball in her hands. "Raw soybeans are a whole lot better than the glop they make at Vitality."

Darby dodged backwards, got into a stance, fired a long jump shot, and made it. "See?" she said. "Who's got more energy, you or me? And anyway, Vitality's foods have a *lot* of soybeans in them."

"Yeah," he said, making another unsuccessful lunge, "but what they do to all those little beans is a crime. Mash 'em up, stew 'em down, then squinch 'em into little rubbery pads."

Justin said, "But boy, they taste good."

"So do M&Ms," Kirk shot back. He made a third lunge, and Darby dodged him and made another basket. He came to a panting stop. "So what are we doing playing basketball when there's all this bad news you got me here for?" he asked.

Darby got around in front of him and looked him in the eye. "Kirkie."

"What?"

"Can I trust you?"

"What do you mean, can you trust me? Trust me with what?"

"With my bad news."

He looked at her closely. Suddenly his jaw fell. "Don't tell me. That CD."

She nodded. "It's gone."

"Darb, I *told* you it was going to be trouble. I *told* you to keep it safe."

"Skip the 'I told you's," she said impatiently. "If you two guys hadn't rattled me by coming into Papa's office and scaring me the way you did, everything would still be under control. The main thing is that the CD's gone. And if we don't find it, I'm really in trouble. And not just me. A whole lot of other people too."

Together she and Justin told the whole story, ending with Justin's careful search of the Heritage Room.

Kirk shrugged. "Only one thing to do," he said. "Turn it over to Justin's dad. He's a detective."

"Used to be," Justin said.

"Not so fast," Darby said. "I don't want any adults knowing that the CD is lost."

"Why not?" Kirk asked.

"Because somebody'll tell somebody else, and pretty soon they'll tell Papa, and he'll want to know what's on it. Don't you see," she said heatedly, "that the main thing we have to do is to keep the CD secret? It's a ticking bomb. We've got to get it back ourselves."

"But until we know who took it—" Kirk began.

"Justin," Darby said, looking Justin in the eye. "If your dad were here, what would be the first thing he'd do?"

Justin grinned. "Poke you on the nose and say 'Vitey-vitey-poo'," he said.

She frowned. "Why do you and your mom keep saying 'poo'? It's 'foo,' not 'poo.' You probably changed it to 'poo' in your crib just because you liked to spit food across the room."

"It's *'poo,'*" Justin insisted. "I remember."

Kirk snorted restlessly. "Foo, poo, who cares?" he asked. "That's not the point. But hey," he said, a hopeful light coming into his eyes, "if we hashed out the foo-poo thing on the Underside Web site, I'd get 700 words out of that, wouldn't I? Especially if we got a lot of e-mail from Darby's mother fans."

"Cut it out, Kirkie."

Kirk sighed. "Go ahead, Justin. Tell us what your dad would do if he took this on as a case."

"I guess," Justin said thoughtfully, "he'd try to figure out who all wants the CD, and how badly they want it. And how possible it was for them to get it."

"Makes sense," Kirk said.

"Molly Jenkins," said a loudspeaker somewhere on the outside wall of the hotel. *"Telephone for Molly Jenkins."*

"Ignore it," Darby said.

Justin looked at her, puzzled. "I was planning to," he said. "There's nobody here named Molly Jenkins."

"Oh, I forgot you didn't know," she said. "Molly Jenkins is the code name the front desk uses when I get a call."

"How come you need a code name?" he asked.

"Think, detective," she said. "Right now all those cheek-pinching mothers are attending a cooking seminar somewhere in the hotel. If they kept hearing 'Call for Darby Joylander,' they wouldn't be able to concentrate on their class. They'd slip out of the room, gather in

packs, and hunt me down and pinch my cheeks."

"We're wasting time," Kirk said. "Who do you think would like to get their hands on that CD?"

"Great-grandma Cora," Darby said promptly. "She knows I'm getting too big to bully around. So if she had the CD to hold over my head, I might not get as stubborn about the Teenage Darby project."

"But how could she use it against you?" Justin wanted to know. "She wouldn't show it anywhere, would she?"

Darby shook her head. "She'd just tell Papa about it, and threaten to send him back to the sales department. Like I said, he *hates* sales."

"Telephone for Molly Jenkins," said the loudspeaker again.

"Maybe your dad's got the CD," Kirk suggested.

Darby turned pale again. "Don't say that."

"He was driving the Energy Express. He could have seen it on the floor and reached down and scooped it up. It had your name on it."

"True," Justin said, "but it had PRIVATE written on it too. Wouldn't he respect that and just give it back to you?"

She shook her head. "Papa's always careful about what I get involved in, especially since Mama's not here. He might just go ahead and pop the CD into the nearest computer to make sure I wasn't downloading something questionable off the Internet." A tear glistened at the corner of her eye. "And if he saw what's *really* on it, it would be like a kick in the stomach to him. He and Mama tried to raise me so healthily, and here I go making jokes about Billy's Bigger Burgers and liking pork even more than hamburgers and lobster. And there's lots of other stuff in the program even worse than that. It's pretty awful, really."

"Molly Jenkins, you have a very urgent phone call," the voice over the loudspeaker said. *"If you're in the building, please respond."*

Darby's eyes turned fearful. "That might be Papa on the line," she said, "telling me he's got the CD."

"Better take the call," Kirk said. "We'll wait for you, and if you don't come back we'll let ourselves out."

She nodded and walked slowly toward the door leading into the hotel, all her energy gone.

"Well," Kirk said after she'd gone, "if her dad's got it, that's better than some others I could think of. Like Wayne Gimble."

"Wait," Justin said. "How could Mr. Gimble have—" Suddenly he gasped. "That's right. He was on the tour too!"

"You bet he was," Kirk agreed, "right there on the Energy Express. He could have seen it lying on the Heritage Room floor just like anybody else. And just think of what he and his BIBI gang could do with the Billy's Burger's part."

Justin's stomach felt sick, as though he'd been eating raw soybeans all week.

Darby was back in less than five minutes. Both boys anxiously studied her face.

"This is all very weird," she said. "I'm not sure what to think."

"Who was it?" Justin asked.

"I don't know," she said. "It was a mysterious voice.

Sort of foreign, maybe Asian."

"Man or woman?" Justin asked. He reached into his beltpack and came out with a small black notebook.

"I couldn't tell," she said. "It was either a man with a high voice or a woman with a low voice. Whoever it was sounded friendly, as if they were smiling."

"Well," Kirk demanded, "what did they say?"

She spoke almost in a whisper. "I said hello, and the voice said, 'Is this Darby Joylander?' and I said yes, and the voice said, 'Miss Joylander, I wanted to let you know that I have your CD. It is safe. I have a favor I would like you to do for me, and I will call again in a half hour.'"

CHAPTER 7

Darby in Disguise

Kirk's eyebrows came together. "Wally does a good Asian accent."

Darby stared. "The Underside Webmaster?"

"Right," he said. "But Wally wouldn't—" and then he stopped short.

"Yes he would, Kirkie," Darby said. "You *know* he would. He'd have my presentation humming over Internet satellites before you could say 'dot-com.'"

"Then why would he call you up wanting a favor from you?"

"Who knows?" she said. "You and he are always looking for the 'underside' of things. Maybe he wants me to tell him some of Vitality's secrets. And anyway," she demanded, "how would he have gotten hold of it? Was he on the tour too?"

Kirk shook his head. "No. But wait. Justin."

Justin looked up from the notes he was making. "What?"

"Did you notice a girl—about 19—short red hair, dressed totally in black?"

Justin thought a moment. "I think I saw somebody like that when we were walking toward the factory. Really pale face."

Kirk nodded. "I saw her too. Agatha. Wally's girlfriend."

"I don't believe this," Darby moaned. "Nobody knew I was going to lose that CD this afternoon, yet that tour was just *loaded* with possible bad guys."

"Just rotten luck," Kirk said. "And I guess it's logical that a lot of people would be here. Today's the first day of the cooking seminars. Vitality is one of the biggest veggie-food makers in the country and it draws a lot of people, good and bad. There's the big merger talks coming up—Thursday morning, I think. And Mr. Gimble naturally wants to keep an eye on the competition, and so does BIBI. And even though Aggie looks like a vampire most of the time, she's a squeaky-clean vegetarian, so I'm sure she's here for the classes. She could have seen that CD and taken it to Wally just to find out what was on it."

"You say the voice is calling back in half an hour?" Justin was still making careful notes in his notebook. "What you need to do is to get the person to talk as much as possible."

Darby shuddered. "Why?"

"The more they talk, the more clues they might give you about who they are."

"So how am I going to get them to talk a lot?"

"Easy," Justin said. "Tell them to prove to you that they have the CD. Have them describe what's on it."

Kirk nodded his head. "Good thinking, Justin."

Darby's eyebrows came together in puzzlement. "But they *must* have the CD. Otherwise why would they have called?"

"I know," Justin said, "but just stall them until you can

get more of a feel about them. Here." He handed her his notebook. "Take this. Get them to give you details. Write down everything they say. And after the phone call's over, just sit there for a few minutes and make sure you copied everything as exactly as you can." He glanced at his watch. "Whoa. I've got to get to the hotel. Dad wants me back by 6:00."

* * *

When Justin made it up to Room 422, Robbie was watching TV and Dad was online with the laptop.

"Where's Mom?" Justin asked.

"You mean the Vivacious VVF Cook?" Robbie asked. "I don't know. But one thing I'm sure of. With hubby so happy, her life is serene."

"Hey, guys," Dad murmured between mouse clicks, "let's ease up on Mom a little. She's not taking this too well."

"Does anybody know where she is?" Justin asked again.

Dad chuckled. "This Volunteer Queen stuff is turning out to be a bigger deal than we thought. Your mom wanted to attend a lot of the cooking seminars this week, but when she went to the first one this afternoon, they brought her up front and congratulated and interviewed her. And you know how much she *loves* talking up front. And it's probably going to be the same at all the other classes she goes to. So," he said firmly, "if you value your life, go easy."

"But it's so much fun," Robbie said with a sigh.

"Back off," Dad commanded.

Fortunately, the room had separate phone lines for the Internet and the phone, because Dad was still Web surfing when the telephone rang.

"I'll get it," Justin said quickly, and grabbed for the receiver. "Hello?"

"Justin, listen." It was Kirk. "When are you having supper?"

"Maybe in 15 minutes."

"Where?"

"Downstairs in Mother's Kitchen."

Kirk's voice took on a disapproving tone. "You mean the Den of Iniquity?" he said. "Do you have any idea what Mother's Kitchen's fried food does to the lining of your stomach?"

Justin interrupted him as tactfully as he could. "Did Darby get her call?"

"She sure did. And we want to talk to you about it. And since you're going to Mother's Den of Iniquity to eat," Kirk said with a sigh, "Darb and I will be in a corner booth. Keep an eye out for us."

"What about the cheek-pinchers?"

Robbie glanced around from the TV with raised eyebrows.

"Darb has this cool wig," Kirk said. "And dark glasses. She'll look like somebody who just got here from France. Remember to call her Celeste."

"Celeste?" Justin said. "This I've gotta see."

When he hung up, Robbie glanced around at him again. "Why is your life so much more interesting than mine?" he said moodily. "What's all this about cheek-pinchers? And who's Celeste?"

"Cheek-pinchers?" Dad suddenly got alert. "Did somebody mention cheek-pinchers?"

"Mr. Case," his older son asked earnestly, "do you really know everything your baby boy is doing behind your back?"

"I'm not doing anything," Justin sputtered.

"Tell me about the cheek-pinchers," Dad said. "Is it a club of some kind?"

Justin quickly explained Darby's problem with adoring mothers, but didn't say anything about the Celeste disguise and the supper meeting.

"I sure would like to meet little Darby," Dad said softly.

"The daughter you never had," Robbie said.

Dad sighed. "Yes, the daughter I never had."

"I'll bet you were hoping Justin would be a girl, weren't you?" Robbie continued.

Dad's voice became instantly alert again. "Oh no," he said quickly. "We were delighted with Justin. We were delighted with both of you."

"We could have Justin dress up like a girl once in awhile if that would help," Robbie suggested.

"Robbie, quit it," Justin said. "When do we eat?"

Dad punched a couple of key combinations on his laptop and the screen faded to dark gray. He glanced at his watch and got to his feet. "Let's eat now," he said. "I guess Mom will have to meet us down there. It's sad to think of her still in that seminar room, surrounded by women wanting her favorite recipes and her autograph."

"Yeah," Robbie said. "They probably think she's smiling when she's really grinding her teeth."

Down in Mother's Kitchen another server, this time younger and with a little red bow in her short brown curls, strolled up to their table and claimed to be Mother's little helper.

"How's Mother doing?" Robbie asked her cheerfully.

"Great," she said. "Are you ready to order?"

"How old is Mother getting to be these days?" he continued.

She smiled nervously. "I don't know. May I—"

"Robbie," Dad said mildly.

"—take your order?" the server finished, giving Dad a grateful look.

While they were waiting for their food, Justin scanned the large room. It wasn't long before he saw Kirk enter. With him was an elegant young woman with short black hair, wearing a black dress and humungous sunglasses. Kirk escorted her to a corner table.

"Dad," Justin said, "there's Kirk. May I go eat with him?"

Dad glanced over at the corner table. "OK, but stay close by." Suddenly his eyes widened, and his head swung quickly around for another glance. "And don't leave the room with that girl in black. We'll send Mother's little helper over with your food."

"Who," Robbie breathed, "is *that?*"

"Mother's little helper?" Dad inquired. "You met her. She took our order."

"No, no," Robbie said. "At the corner table."

Dad grinned. "Cool your jets. It's too late to cancel your college year in Australia."

"She must be what—17?" Robbie murmured.

"Sixteen," Dad said. "Looks European. Probably a visiting countess who loves veggie food."

Though it was killing him, Justin kept an absolutely straight face until he was seated at the corner table. Then he broke into a spasm of giggling. "My brother thinks you're 17!" he chortled to Darby. "But when he saw you at the hotel door this morning in your pink dress he thought you were 10. Cool disguise."

"Ooh-la-la," said Darby loudly with a mysterious French smile. Under her breath she said, "I got the call. And like you said, I tried to keep him talking."

"It was a he?"

"Oui, oui," Darby said loudly, and whispered. "Don't laugh at me when I'm trying to talk French. If you blow my cover and the cheek-pinchers get me, I'll never forgive you."

Kirk suddenly sat up alertly. "Justin," he said, "your brother is coming over here."

"Run, Darby," urged Justin.

"The name's Celeste," she hissed back. "I'll take care of him."

Robbie sauntered up to the table. "Hi," he said in a deep voice.

"Hi," Kirk and Justin said nervously, almost together.

"May I be introduced to your friend?"

"Ooh-la-la," Justin said. "I mean, yes. This is Celeste."

Darby looked down, fumbled with her purse, then said coolly, *"Les cheveux sont ainsi renforces de la racine."* She glanced downward again, then added, *"Aux pointes en seulement dix jours."*

"I am pleased to meet you too," Robbie replied gallantly. "Have you been in this country long?"

"Appliquez sur les cheveux mouilles," Darby said in an even more chilly voice, *"apres le shampooing fortifiant."*

"Ooh-la-la," said Robbie a little uncertainly. "Well, I hope you have a nice stay. I'll see you around." He bowed slightly, turned, and walked back across the room.

Both boys laughed as hard and as silently as they could. Then Kirk said, "I didn't know you spoke French, Darb."

"And," said Justin, "I didn't know my brother understood it."

"Oui, oui," Darby said with a brilliant smile. Then in a low voice she said, "I can't speak French. It's stuff printed on the back of a little hotel shampoo bottle that has instructions in French and English. I had it in my purse."

Justin giggled. "What does it mean?"

"From what I read on the bottle, the first sentence is something about how hair is strengthened from roots to ends in just 10 days. The second one tells you to apply the shampoo to wet hair. Hey, stop laughing," she told Justin earnestly. "Your brother is going to look at us and think I'm a boxload of fun after all, and come back over here and pretend to understand some more hair advice."

"The phone call," Kirk said. "Tell Justin about the call."

Darby fumbled around in her thin black French purse and pulled out Justin's notebook. "I wrote it all down like you said." She gazed at her notes for a moment. "I don't think things are as bad as we thought. But this is going to sound really bizarre."

CHAPTER 8

The Wall Drug Strategy

"The caller had a kind voice," Darby continued, "and he sounded really embarrassed. He said that he was a close friend of one of Papa's clients. He called the client Mr. Wong, but he said that wasn't his real name. This Mr. Wong is an Asian businessman who imports a lot of Vitality food across the Pacific Ocean."

Justin leaned forward. "So what did the caller want?"

"Here's what he said," Darby replied, lowering her voice. "About a year ago Mr. Wong came over here to visit Vitality. He gave Papa a present—a little jade statue of Buddha about this high." She held her hand about eight inches above the table. "It's in Papa's office on a shelf on the wall. I've seen it lots of times. A cute little bald guy with a big tummy, carved out of green stone, sitting there staring at Papa."

"I don't blame him," Kirk said.

"Don't blame who?" Justin asked.

"I don't blame the statue for being green," Kirk said firmly. "If I had to stare at Darby's papa all day, knowing what his company does to the innocent soybean, *I'd* turn green too."

Darby lifted her sunglasses for an instant and gave him

an icy French glare. "And now back to our regularly sched-
uled program," she said, lowering the glasses. "It turns out
that the caller was visiting Papa's office not too long ago.
He went over to the shelf and picked up the Buddha statue.
Suddenly he saw that the statue had a serious flaw in it,
some sort of dark streak running through the stone that
isn't supposed to be there."

"So why bring you into it?" Kirk asked.

"The caller phoned Mr. Wong and told him about the
flaw," said Darby, glancing at the notebook. "Mr. Wong was
really embarrassed. And now he wants me to switch the
bad Buddha for a good one exactly like it."

Justin blinked. "Why doesn't the caller just make an ap-
pointment with your dad?"

"I guess it's a matter of honor or pride or something,"
Darby said. "Mr. Wong doesn't want word to get out that he
carelessly gives flawed presents to valued friends. Maybe
that's a big no-no in his culture, even if it was just a mistake."

Kirk scowled. "What I don't like is that they're holding
your CD hostage."

She shook her head. "I don't think they're really holding
it hostage. I think he just found it and he's keeping it for me."

Justin shook his head. "I agree with Kirk. Sounds like a
bribe to me. Did you ask him to prove he really has the CD?"

She nodded. "He was really nice about it. He described
all sorts of things on it. Here are the notes I wrote down."
She cleared her throat and began to read aloud. "'He told
about my pretending to like pork best of all, and about how
I pretend that Papa took me on a deer-hunting trip and that

Mama taught me how to cook opossum. He told about how I cried because I wanted a second Billy's Bigger Burger.'"

Kirk slumped in discouragement. "Well, I guess he's got it then," he said. "How does he want to make the switch?"

"You know the Wall Drug bus trip?"

Justin, who had been making some notes on a napkin, glanced up with a blank stare. "The *what* trip?"

"It's tomorrow," she said. "For people who want to go, Vitality's taking a couple of buses over to Wall Drug. It's about an hour and a half from here."

"But there's a drugstore a whole lot closer than that," Justin said. "It's over by the mall, like a mile away. I saw it as we drove in."

Darby's eyebrows rose. "You've never heard of Wall Drug?" she asked in amazement.

"Nope."

Kirk offered him his right hand. "Finally," he said, peering over his tiny glasses, "a human being with a pure and uncluttered mind."

Justin glanced from one to the other. "What are you guys talking about?" he asked.

"Wall Drug," Kirk told him solemnly, "is South Dakota's most popular tourist trap."

"That's right," Darby agreed. She suddenly remembered that she was supposed to be French, and tossed off another short shampoo bottle instruction with a brilliant smile.

"Ooh-la-la," Kirk replied thoughtfully, and then turned to Justin. "Let's just say that not a lot of people stop at Wall Drug to get their prescriptions filled."

"OK," Justin said. "But what does Wall Drug have to do with the Buddha thing?"

Darby lowered her voice. "That's where I'm supposed to make the switch."

"And Justin and I are coming along, of course," Kirk said.

Darby shook her head. "No, it's got to be just me."

"How come?"

"Because," she said, "that's what the caller said. He said someone would be watching."

Kirk frowned. "Darb," he said, "I don't like this."

"Neither do I," Justin agreed.

"Look," she replied, "it's probably OK. I'll just grab the Buddha tomorrow morning, take it to Wall Drug, make the switch, and be back on the bus for the trip home."

"Wait a minute," Justin said. "How do we know that this whole thing isn't just a plot to steal a real jade Buddha and put a fake one in its place? In that case you'd be part of a burglary plot."

She stared at him with large eyes, and nodded. "I thought about that," she said, "but I've got no choice. I mean, it's not like Papa *bought* that Buddha. It doesn't mean anything to him. He's always getting presents like that, and most of them he just puts in glass cases in a display room."

Kirk shrugged. "Maybe she's right," he said.

"No," Justin said, "you can't just cave in to the caller that way. Look, I've got an idea."

* * *

And Justin's idea was the reason that a rather bewildered Case family happened to be sitting in one of the huge, plush Vitality Vegetarian Foods buses the next morning as it pulled away from the parking lot.

"All I want to know," Robbie growled from behind his *Traveler's Guide to Australia,* "is why I am here."

"We need to expose you to some South Dakota culture, my boy," Dad murmured. "Soon you're going to be down under, dodging kangaroos and boomerangs. Wall Drug will provide the perfect balance for you. Tove, you agree with me, don't you?" he said anxiously to Mom.

Tovah Case was surprisingly cheerful. "Agreed," she said. "Balance is good. We all need balance. And I," she said firmly, "need to be away from those cooking seminars for the day. Justin, thank you for insisting that we come."

"You're welcome." Justin gave a silent sigh of relief as he saw them all sitting in a row. "And there's another thing."

"What's that?" Mom said, smiling warmly.

Justin paused. Mom's sudden change in attitude made life a lot brighter. But he wasn't sure whether the change had happened only because she wouldn't have to be interviewed in front of cooking seminar audiences today. Was there something else too? He gave an anxious glance at her, and then said, "Dad will get to meet Darby."

Mom's smile broadened. "That's right, he will, won't he?"

"Darby? Is she on the bus too?" Dad looked quickly around him.

"I'll go get her," Justin said, and hurried to the front of the bus, where Darby was talking with the driver. "Darby, could you come and meet my family?"

Darby wasn't wearing her French outfit, but she wasn't in pink either. She wore jeans and a blue top, and had pulled her golden Shirley Temple hair firmly back behind her ears. She followed him to the back of the bus.

"Hello, Darby," Mom said with a warm smile.

Dad gave a cuddly chuckle. "Hi there, little lady."

She grinned. "Hi, Mr. Case. Nice to meet you."

"Vitey-vitey-poo," he chuckled.

"Vitey-vitey-foo," she chuckled back.

"We sure enjoyed those little commercials of yours," he said. "You made a big hit with my son."

"No stories, Dad," Justin warned.

"Oh, Mr. Case, please tell me some stories," Darby said in her most enchanting voice, ignoring Justin's scowl.

"Sure," Dad said. "The one I remember best involved mashed peas."

Justin gasped with horror. "Dad! Not that!"

"Or anyway, they *looked* like mashed peas," Dad said. "It was some sort of baby food that came in a glass jar."

"How fascinating," Darby breathed, her eyes fixed on his face.

"Dad, please," Justin moaned. He put both hands over his ears.

"Our baby boy was probably 3 at the time," he heard Dad say faintly through his plugged ears. "And we did not realize at that time that young Jelly Face had learned how to unscrew jar lids."

"Don't call me Jelly Face," Justin groaned. His voice

sounded huge and booming inside his head.

"There was no other name that fit you better at that stage in your life," Dad reminded him. "You loved jelly, and you wanted it as close to you as possible. After you'd eaten your peanut-butter-and-jelly sandwich and spat some of it on your high chair and on several bystanders, you always smeared what was left on your face." Dad laid his hand lovingly on his son's arm. Justin shook it off like a snake. "But as I was saying," his father continued, "you—"

"Dad," Justin said desperately, "may Darby and I ask you a question in private?"

"No," Robbie said from behind the *Traveler's Guide,* "you can't get married. Not at Wall Drug, at least. Drugstore marriages aren't legal, and research says they don't last very long anyway."

Justin and Darby both blushed.

Dad grinned. "Believe it or not, Wall Drug does have a little chapel," he chuckled.

Darby's blush suddenly faded, and her eyes grew wide. She stared at Dad, then glanced at her watch. "You're right about the chapel," she said. "And that's part of what we needed to talk to you about. But please don't forget to finish your story later," she begged.

"I promise," Dad said, as he got to his feet. "We'll have a bit more privacy a couple of rows back," he murmured. "Actually, a bus isn't the best place to tell the mashed peas story. You need a lot of space for gestures, and for dodging Justin's blows."

Darby slid into the window seat and Dad sat beside

her. Justin crouched in the aisle. "OK, kids," Dad said briskly. "There's been enough mystery about why it's so desperately necessary that we go to Wall Drug today. Fill me in."

As Darby quickly sketched out the story, Justin saw his Dad's face change. And when she got to the end, his eyes were narrow and watchful.

"Well, well," he said. He glanced casually around him, then bent his head near Darby's. "Do you recognize anyone on this bus besides us?"

She shook her head quickly. "No."

"Any Asian people who might be your caller?"

"I doubt it. I'm not sure."

"Is there anybody on the bus who's been watching you closely or paying special attention to you?"

She shook her head again. "I don't think so."

"Where's your friend Kirk?"

"He's going to meet us at Wall Drug," she said.

Justin suddenly asked, "How's he getting there?"

"It's OK," she said. "He got Wally to drop him off there to do some Underside research." She glanced at her watch again and said timidly, "We're almost there. We need to make some decisions."

CHAPTER 9

Eye of the Buddha

"We're in a tough situation," Mr. Case pointed out. "On the one hand, we don't know whom we're dealing with, and we might be helping commit a crime. On the other hand, you say that if the CD gets publicized it could hurt you and your family and probably Vitality."

"I'm sure of it," she said in a small voice.

"So what do you want me to do?"

"What I was hoping was this," Darby said quickly. "I'll go into the chapel and make the switch—that's where the person told me to go. And I'll bring the new Buddha out to you and you can take a look at it. If you see something suspicious, I could just take it into the chapel and switch it back again." She swallowed. "And we'd all just have to live with whatever happens."

Dad suddenly grinned. "You're a brave young lady. I remember watching you on those commercials and thinking, *This girl's got spunk. Anybody who can take the phrase 'Vitality Vegetarian Foods' and make it immortal is tops in my book.* He sighed, and reverently repeated, "Vitey-vitey-poo."

"Foo," she said.

Dad glanced at her alertly. *"Foo?* I thought it was *poo."*

"Foo."

"Then why," he asked earnestly, "did Tovah and I have to keep scraping so much raspberry jam off our wallpaper? I say it was poo."

"Dad," Justin said, "back to the point."

Dad sighed. "OK. Since you're supposed to make the Buddha switch alone, Darby, I can't be anywhere visible. And you can't be seen meeting with me."

"I've got a plan," she said.

"So do I," said Dad. "Let's compare them." And the three of them spoke together in low voices.

* * *

Justin studied the town of Wall as the bus approached it. "What's so great about Wall Drug?" he asked Darby. "There are all these huge signs on the freeway that talk about it, but it doesn't look like much."

Darby pointed. "Except for that dinosaur beside the freeway."

"Why the dinosaur?" Justin asked.

"Wall Drug has everything. Everything you don't need, and lots of it. But I think it's sweet."

Justin gave her a doubtful sideways glance. "You think Wall Drug is *sweet?*"

"Sweet," she repeated firmly, then added with a smile, "just like me."

After the bus had nosed its way into a parking lot, Darby and the Case family strolled toward the town's main street, where loads of other tourists were swarming.

"Hey, there's Kirk," Justin said. The thin boy was staring into an open doorway.

"You're right," Darby said. "Mr. Case, I've thought of a place for you. You can go sit beside Mount Rushmore."

Dad shot her a puzzled glance. "Mount Rushmore is a hundred miles away."

She laughed. "No, I mean the Mount Rushmore model out in the backyard of Wall Drug. People go stand behind it and look through the holes where the presidents' faces usually are, and get their picture taken."

"Gotcha," Dad said. "I'll go find it now." And he disappeared through the open doorway. Then he stuck his head out. "Hey, don't miss what's going on inside here. There are some wooden singing cowboys!" He vanished again.

"OK," said Darby briskly to Justin. "Kirkie's going to take you to get your face painted."

Justin stared. "My face? Painted?"

"Sure," Kirk said. "Darby's supposed to be here alone, right?"

"Yeah, but why the paint?"

"Because," Darby said, "anybody hanging around the Vitality Resort Hotel might have seen the three of us together. So you've got to disguise yourselves." She glanced at her watch. "In 30 minutes I'll go into the chapel. You can hang around and help tourists and also check to see if anyone's following me."

"Will do," said Kirk. "Let's go, Justin."

Justin's head was spinning as Kirk hurried him in through the door of Wall Drug. To their left, behind glass, was a group of life-size wooden singing cowboys, limbs jerking and mouths moving, while loudspeakers blared out an old-time cowboy song. Beside them, a fake dog scratched himself, and a fake hen laid the same egg over and over again.

Justin would have stayed to watch this fascinating scene, but Kirk kept him moving.

"What's all this about, Kirk?" Justin said. "Why do we have to help tourists?"

"So that we'll have a reason for hanging around outside the chapel," Kirk said over his shoulder. "Wall Drug has a great summer program where high school students come and work. We're a little younger than that, but we should fit in OK."

"But how many tourists are going to ask for help from somebody with a painted face?" Justin protested. "And anyway, I don't know anything about Wall Drug. How can I help anybody?"

"Hurry," Kirk said. "You be a chief; I'll be a brave."

And before Justin knew what was happening, a cheerful high school girl was slapping colorful Native American paint on his face.

"Take your shirt off," she commanded.

Justin's eyes bugged out. "I'm not taking my—"

"We've got lockers over there," she said. "Got to get you all painted up, front and back."

"I don't believe this!" Justin squawked.

"You don't?" Kirk said. "Then let me take this quick picture of you." His digital camera blinked. "Now you can cher-

ish the memory forever. And I can do 700 words for
Underside on how today's young people are exploring
Native American culture firsthand. Whoa, Justin," he said
as soon as their disguise was complete. "You look really
cool. Hey, don't glare like that. Remember, you're a tourist
helper. Here's a brochure."

Justin's scowl smoothed out a bit. "So what do we do?"

"Come on," Kirk said, threading his way past counters
filled with souvenirs such as bronze cowboy statues and
stuffed horses and back scratchers and fake buffalo dung.
"We're going to hang around the hallway just outside the
chapel. And when we see tourists with blank looks on their
faces, we ask them if we can give them directions. But first,
say 'How.'"

"How?"

"Like this. 'How,'" Kirk said, pronouncing it clearly.

"No, I mean why 'how'?"

"No, not 'why how,' just 'how.'"

Justin glared. "No, I mean, why do we have to say 'how'?"

"Beats me," Kirk said with a shrug. "People used to
think it was a Native American greeting. It probably wasn't,
but tourists think it is. Try it."

"How," Justin said darkly.

"With a smile."

"How with a smile," Justin said.

"Justin!" Kirk said in an exasperated voice.

Justin suddenly grinned. "I'm kidding," he said. "OK,
let's go."

The hallway outside the chapel doorway was noisy.

Dozens of tourists stared at paintings on the wall, or drifted in and out of little stores. Kids got their pictures taken sitting on the lap of a wooden pioneer cowboy seated on a bench. Down at one end of the hall was a shooting gallery where three or four kids tried their luck.

Justin and Kirk began how-ing their way up and down the hall. Little kids stared at them in amazement, and if the two fake Native Americans spoke to them they squeaked in delight.

Exactly when she'd said she would, Darby appeared, walking casually along the hall carrying a large paper bag. She slipped into the chapel. A few seconds later Justin how'd his way over to where he could see inside.

The chapel was long and narrow with stained-glass windows up next to a high ceiling. Way up at the front, past the rows of pews, Darby was crouching by the altar. Justin saw her lean quickly forward and reach behind and inside it. He heard the brief rustle of bag-paper. A few moments later she got to her feet.

Justin turned, saw an elderly couple coming by, how'd them, and asked them if he could be of help. As he chatted with them, he turned so he could watch Darby depart.

Once the couple had gone, Kirk drifted over to compare notes. "I didn't see anyone follow her. Doesn't seem like the caller is bothering to check up on her. He probably knows how bad she wants that CD kept quiet, and figures she won't foul things up. None of this would have happened," he said with a disapproving frown, "if Darby had been eating her daily dose of raw soybeans—she would have been more stable."

"Do the lecture later," Justin suggested. "Lead me to Mount Rushmore."

Kirk hurried Justin through room after room, past tourists' elbows and purses, out through a hallway, across a back alley, and into a yard filled with lots of things, such as a giant jackrabbit and a huge gorilla with its right arm raised.

"Mount Rushmore," Kirk said, pointing.

A large gray model of the famous mountain stood before them. The faces of Washington, Jefferson, Lincoln, and Roosevelt weren't there, though. Instead, there were four hollow ovals. While they watched, Jefferson's oval turned from dark to tan, and Dad's face peered anxiously out. His eyes darted left and right.

Justin giggled. "He doesn't recognize us."

The two of them hurried back behind the wooden mountain. Darby and Dad were crouching together, and Dad was staring into her paper bag. When he saw the two boys approaching, he gulped and clutched the bag to his chest. Then his detective instincts caused his eyes to narrow.

"You *guys,*" he said, taking a deep breath. "You've gotta be kidding."

"Disguise," Kirk said quickly. "What's happening, Mr. Case?"

"We've got to be quick," Darby cut in. "Here, let's move back a little. A family's coming back here to get their picture taken."

The tourist family stared curiously at the strange little

council between two Native Americans and two White people. Justin and Kirk how'd the tourist kids, who stepped away uncertainly.

Meanwhile, Dad was studying as much of the new jade Buddha as he could see by looking into the top of the paper sack. He turned his back on the tourists and drew it out of its bag, turning it this way and that way.

"Not quite heavy enough," he said. "But my Internet research indicates that this is real jade. Might be hollowed out inside."

"I didn't see any flaws in the old one," Darby said. "Let's compare them."

Kirk stared. "Compare them? Didn't you leave the original back in the chapel like the caller said to?"

She grinned and shook her head. "It was Mr. Case's idea not to."

"But what's the caller going to do when he doesn't find it?"

Dad chuckled. "There's not much he can do. The main thing he wants is for the new Buddha to be in Don Joylander's office. And I have a suspicion about why." He peered closely at the new Buddha. "Aha," he said. "Look at the eye."

They bent their heads over the image.

Kirk said, "It looks like the left one's shinier than the right one."

"Excellent observation," Dad said. "You're right."

"But what does it mean?" Darby asked.

Dad smiled. "I had a strong suspicion it was something like this. It's espionage."

"Spying?" Justin asked.

Dad nodded. "What we have here"—and he tapped the Buddha—"is a high-tech video camera, complete with microphone."

CHAPTER 10

Somebody's Been Listening

The kids stared at him, mouths open.

"Why?" Darby asked.

"The merger," Justin suddenly said.

Dad nodded. "Any one of those other big veggie-food businesses—or maybe even this Asian client, if he's real—would be really, really interested to learn who Donald Joylander talks with in his office. And what amounts of money they talk about."

"And Wayne Gimble, too," Kirk broke in. "If Vitality's products are cutting into the beef business, Gimble would for sure want to listen in on any planning."

"And Great-grandma Cora," Darby said. "She's another one who might be planting this Buddha. She doesn't trust Papa. She's always looking for an excuse to get him back into sales."

Justin spoke up again. "But why would she go to all this trouble to have someone call Darby on the phone? Why wouldn't she just walk into the office and switch the Buddha herself?"

Dad shrugged. "She might want it to look like an outside job if somebody discovers what it really is."

"Wally, too," Kirk gulped, staring at the Buddha's shiny

MMM-4

eye. "This is just the kind of high-tech gadget he'd come up with. *Whoa,*" he whispered, backing away. "I just thought of something. If this is a video camera, whoever it belongs to is probably listening and watching us right now."

Dad shook his head. "I don't think it's turned on. For one thing, it would wear the battery down. Also, this is probably a transmitter, and the pickup unit would have to be pretty close by for them to get a good signal. I think it's going to be activated by some sort of electronic radio signal once it's in Don Joylander's office, maybe from a van in the parking lot."

Darby whispered, "And they'll probably check that it's working before they give me my CD back."

Dad nodded. "Yes, by activating it and seeing if they can pick up anything on their monitors." He slid the Buddha back into the paper bag, where it clinked against the other one, and handed the bag to Darby. "There you are," he said. "You go first, and we'll trail you. Walk naturally. See you on the bus."

* * *

"Something is bothering me," said Justin.

His voice was muffled by the Vitality Foods veggie-burger he was munching on. He and Kirk, still in their forehead-to-belly-button paint, were huddled together with Darby in the very back seat of the Vitality bus, which was now on the freeway rolling toward home. "By the way, thanks for the burger, Darby."

She grinned. "Wall Drug's giving them a trial run in their restaurant. They say people love them. What's bothering you?"

"Probably that mangled soy product," Kirk broke in. But he was staring at Justin's burger with a look of longing.

"Here, Kirkie," Darby said, whipping a paper bag from behind her. "I got you one too."

His mouth fell open. "Darb, you know I don't eat this stuff."

"Come on. I'll bet you've never even tried one." She dropped the bag in his lap.

He swallowed. "Nice try, Darb. But—" his voice faded.

"Smells good, right?"

He stared down at the sack.

"Come on, Kirkie. Veggie food is not a sin."

Justin said, "Just take one bite."

Kirk's eyes were still locked on the sack. "But it's *processed.*"

"Mom says they're making veggie meat a whole lot healthier than they used to," Justin insisted. "Less salt, less fat. All the nutrition newsletters love Vitality's burgers. They get A-pluses everywhere."

"You're hungry, Kirkie, and you know it," Darby said. "Just scarf it down. We won't tell."

"You *guys,*" Kirk said. But then he opened the top of the bag. His eyes closed as a fresh wave of aroma wafted up toward his nostrils. He reached in and pulled out the warm burger.

"The moment of truth," Darby whispered. "You'll love it."

"But the Bible says—" he began.

"—The Bible says that Jesus cooked fish for His disciples after they spent all night on the lake," Justin said. "Clean, nonpolluted fish, of course. There wasn't any industrial waste in the Sea of Galilee. And the Bible does *not* say that Jesus went around carrying a bag of raw soybeans."

Darby nodded. "Healthy living has got to be balanced, Kirkie."

Kirk had raised the burger to his lips and half-opened his mouth. But suddenly he stopped and gave her a level stare. *"Riiight.* Cheese curls in one hand and a soda in the other. That's real balance."

She blushed and dropped her eyes. "Don't rub it in, Kirkie. I'm working on that."

"You're too thin," he said.

"OK, maybe I am."

Justin cleared his throat and held out his hand. "Uh, Kirk, if you don't want that burger . . ."

The other boy glanced at him in alarm. "That's OK," he said quickly. He opened his mouth and took a big bite.

"Yea, Kirkie!" Darby shouted, and Justin slapped him encouragingly on the back.

"Quiet," Kirk choked through the burger bun. "No need to call a news conference."

"Is it good?" she asked excitedly.

He chewed some more. "It's OK," he said, and took two more quick bites.

Darby grinned. "Not too bad for a rubbery little soy patty, is it?"

He avoided her eyes and took another bite.

"Something's bothering me," Justin said.

She glanced at him. "You said that before, Chief Beanburger. What's bothering you?"

He took out his black notebook. "Last night," he said uneasily, "I was reading through the notes you wrote, about when you asked the caller some questions to make sure he had the CD. Kirk, listen up. Something doesn't seem to check out."

Kirk turned dreamy eyes on him, and took another bite of his veggieburger.

"What doesn't check out?" Darby asked.

"I just need some facts cleared up. Here." Justin handed her the notebook. "Read what you wrote. Right there," he said, pointing. "Where the caller describes what was on the CD."

She began reading aloud. " 'He told about my pretending to like pork best of all, and about how I pretend that Papa took me on a deer-hunting trip and that Mama taught me how to cook opossum. He told about—' "

She stopped, and her eyebrows came together in a frown. "Wait, that's not right."

"What's not right?" Kirk said through the final bite of his burger bun.

"Did I write that?" she said, staring closely at the notebook.

"That's what you wrote," Justin said.

"But it's not true."

Justin leaned forward, trying to control the excitement in his voice. "What part of it isn't true?"

She licked her lips nervously. "The part about Mama and the opossum."

"Aha!" Justin said. "Just like I thought."

Kirk looked puzzled. "What isn't true? I can't figure out what you're getting at."

"That veggieburger's rotting your brain already," Darby said, finger-poking him in his painted ribs. Then she turned to Justin. "But I've got my own figuring out to do."

"Look at what you wrote again," he said. "What's not true about it?"

She was very pale. *"There's nothing on that CD about Mama teaching me to cook opossum."*

Kirk wiped his mouth with a napkin. "Yes there is, Darb. You told us about it."

She looked at him. "When?"

"In your dad's office. When Justin and I scared you as you were working on the PowerPoint thing."

Justin nodded. "That's where you mentioned it," he said.

"But—" Darby stopped, and looked from one to the other of them. "But something's really wrong here."

"That's what you wrote, isn't it?" Kirk asked. "About the opossum?"

She looked dazed. "I must have just copied down what the caller said without thinking about it. But if they looked at the CD at all, they didn't find anything about the opossum on it. And that's because—"

Justin's voice trembled. "Why, Darby? Why?"

"Because," she said, "the opossum thing was only in my head, not on the CD. I was working it out in my head."

Justin sighed with relief. "I thought so."

Kirk snorted. "Whoever took your CD isn't a mind-reader, Darb."

"Give me a minute to think," Justin said. "Don't talk, just let me think." He shut his eyes for about 15 seconds. Suddenly they popped open. "There's only one answer to this whole thing," he said.

"What's that?" asked Kirk.

Justin stared at each of them with wide eyes. Then he said, *"The caller and whomever he's working for don't have the CD!"*

Kirk shook his head. "You've got to change to a raw soybean diet, Justin," he said gently. "You're losing it. Just remember the facts, step by step. Darb loses the CD. Someone calls up, telling her he's *got* the CD, and describes a lot of what's on it. Of course he's got the CD. How else would he know it was gone?"

Justin stared straight at him. "He overheard us talking about how it disappeared."

Darby frowned. "Overheard us? Where?"

"He overheard you tell us what was on the CD," Justin said rapidly. "Then he overheard you mention the Mama-opossum thing. But he didn't catch that you hadn't actually recorded it. That's the mistake he made. He's just pretending he's got the CD."

"But where? Where did he hear us?" Darby demanded. "I don't remember talking about it except in Papa's—" she paused, and her eyes got as wide as Justin's. "In Papa's office!"

Justin nodded. "That's the only place we could have been overheard."

"But there was nobody else there."

"Oh yes there was, Darby," he said. "Somewhere in that office is a hidden microphone."

CHAPTER 11

Class Acts

Two hours later three silent kids plus a silent and very wide-eyed Donald Joylander stood in the office and watched as a silent Robert Case crept across the floor in stocking feet. In his hands he held a magnifying glass and a powerful little flashlight.

It took Dad just eight minutes to spot the tiny microphone. When he did, he motioned the others over behind Mr. Joylander's desk. He pointed to the knob on the desk's right-hand top drawer. Then he beckoned them outside the office door and closed it.

"But *why?*" Mr. Joylander exploded. "And *who?*"

Dad shrugged. "Could be any of several people. You could probably come up with a list of suspects longer than mine. Industrial espionage happens all the time. Who knows how long that bug's been there? A maintenance man, a repair person, anybody could have installed it and wired it in half an hour."

"Why didn't you just rip it out?" Mr. Joylander said. "This is criminal! What's behind all this? And where do the kids come into it?"

"Would you do me a favor," Dad asked mildly, "and wait on the answers until after the banquet Thursday night?

We'll probably be able to sort it all out by then."

Mr. Joylander glanced wrathfully back at his office. "But—"

"If you'll just wait," Dad urged him, "we can find out who did it. If not, we may never know. And one more bit of advice," he said. "When you talk about the merger you're planning, don't do it in your office. Use the Mother's Kitchen banquet room or someplace like that."

* * *

"Tove, are you sure you're going to be OK?" Dad asked gently.

It was Thursday night, and the Case family had gathered backstage in the huge ballroom of the Vitality Resort Hotel. Sound technicians and other people were hurrying around them doing last-minute setup. Beyond the stage curtains they could hear a huge audience gathering at tables.

"What time is it?" Mom asked. Over her dress she wore a long, frilly white apron with huge pockets. In her right hand she held a large red rolling pin.

"Just remember, Mom, your life is serene, with hubby so happy, I mean. Hey, that rhymes too!"

"Robbie," Dad warned.

Mom smiled. "That's right," she said calmly, "my life *is* serene."

"Mom," Justin said, "are you feeling . . . OK?"

"I am feeling just fine, Jelly Face," she said.

"I mean, you've been in a really good mood the last

couple of days," he continued.

"Tove, you didn't take tranquilizers or anything like that?" Dad asked anxiously. "I know how difficult this has been for you. I just don't want you to trip and fall off the stage."

"Oh, I'm going to enjoy myself," she said. "Really."

Robbie and Dad and Justin exchanged worried glances.

"Well, that's great," Dad said. "We'll be down there in the front row cheering you on."

"Oh, no you won't," she said in a dreamy voice.

The three men in her life stared at her.

"What?" Robbie asked. "What did you say?"

"You're not going anywhere," she replied, "until Darby gets here."

"Why not?" Justin wanted to know.

"Tovah, we'd be glad to stay backstage to support you," Dad began. "But—"

Robbie finished his sentence. "—but it'll be more fun to watch from out front."

"Here comes Darby," Justin said. "She's got some huge paper bags with her."

Darby was smiling with great delight. She smiled at Mom, and Mom smiled back at her. Then Darby's smile disappeared, and a determined look appeared on her face.

"OK, guys," she said, "here are *your* costumes."

At first none of the three males understood what she meant.

Dad smiled. "Costumes? We're not on the program."

"Oh, but you are, Mr. Case," Darby said sweetly. "And you too, Justin, along with your brother. You're going to be playing the part of an American family who has discovered how happy Vitality foods have made you. Mr. Case, there's a dressing room right there."

"Tovah," Dad said with a numb look on his face, "this was a plot. This is why you've been smiling a lot in the last couple of days."

Mom smiled again, even more widely.

Dad sighed, took his costume bag, and disappeared.

"Robbie, Justin, here you are." Darby handed them each a bag.

They turned pale and stared at each other, and then at Darby.

"Sorry," Robbie said. "Can't do it. Sorry."

Justin shook his head. "Me neither."

"Get those costumes on *now,*" Mom ordered. *"Right now."*

"Mom!" Justin wailed. "I don't want to do this. I don't know what to do!"

"I've got scripts you can read," Darby said briskly. "They're corny, but so are you. Remember? 'Rah-rah-rah.' Now get changed. *Quick.*"

"I don't believe this," Robbie gasped. "I'm not having any part of it."

"Oh yes you are, buddy," his mother told him. "If you back out, I don't get my prize money."

"You love your mother, don't you?" Darby asked sternly.

Robbie's face became as stunned as Dad's. He took his bag and stumbled toward the dressing room.

Justin looked into in his bag. When he glanced up

again, his eyes were wide with horror. "You got the wrong bag!" he choked. "This is a girl's dress!"

She nodded. "Hurry."

"I'm not dressing like a girl!"

"Just slip the dress on over your jeans if you want to," she said. "It's more like a muumuu."

"No!" he cried, then turned away.

Darby came around to where she could look him square in the eye. "Your script has a girl's part, Justin," she said. "There's no time to rewrite it."

"Bite the bullet, Jelly Face," Mom said. "This is your Vivacious VVF Cook speaking." She smiled fondly. "You are going to look *so cute.* Darby showed me your blond wig. If you don't watch out, many a grateful kiss I'll steal."

"I'm not going to wear a wig!"

"Oui-oui," Darby said. "Now get that costume on so the sound guys can get your lapel mikes fixed. Hurry. We're on as soon as my commercial documentary is over." She grinned. "It's the real CD, by the way. I made sure of that."

There weren't any mirrors in the dressing room, so Justin wasn't exactly sure what he looked like. As he struggled into the dress and adjusted the wig, he could hear the huge, recorded voice of Darby chirping away over the sound system. Every once in awhile there was laughter and applause.

But nothing like the laughter I'm going to get, he thought moodily.

And when he opened the door and came out into the backstage area again, he was greeted by muffled screams of delight. His mother and Darby bent double, their hands over their mouths. Robbie, who'd already changed, stared at his younger brother like he had just arrived from Jupiter. Dad, who was wearing 1940s style clothes and hat, was equally amazed.

"The daughter you never had?" Robbie said to him.

Dad tried to keep a straight face. "The daughter I ever had."

"Justin," Mom said through her convulsions of mirth, "you look perfect, sweetheart."

"Like a little Swiss girl in a bad mood," Robbie said.

"But whatever you do," Mom continued, "do *not* look in a mirror."

"Right," Darby said. "We've got to keep your courage up."

They did a quick read-through of the script, and then Darby said, "OK, leave your scripts backstage. There'll be TV monitors to prompt you like they have on the talk shows. Just watch them and wait for your lines, and try to act normal."

Mom took one glance at Justin, and collapsed again with laughter. A fruity-voiced announcer boomed, "And now, ladies and gentlemen, we're going to take you straight into the kitchen of the Rannygazoo family! Let's meet them now—Ralph and Ramona Rannygazoo, and their children, Ricky and Ruthie!"

Justin felt a firm knuckle in his ribs. "Rah-rah, Ruthie," said Darby in his ear. "Dad says a truck from the local TV station's outside. Smile big for the cameras."

The knuckle pushed hard, and Justin stumbled onto

the stage into the blazing white spotlights.

* * *

Justin doesn't remember much of what happened for the next six or seven minutes. In fact, since then he's been trying to forget what he *does* remember. The story line was pretty simple. Ralph and Ramona were the average American couple, eating the average American way—burgers, fries, and other fatty foods.

Ricky was always sick, and Ruthie had problems as well. The only line Justin remembers from the dialogue was where he had to rub his cheek and say, "Oh, these horrid acne zits! What *shall* I do?"

This caused a tremendous roar of laughter, and he gave a worried glance at the audience, trying to spot the TV cameras. He glanced down, and there was Kirk crouching in front of the stage, blinking steadily away with his digital camera.

Fortunately, just before their lives totally collapsed, the Rannygazoo family learned about Vitality Vegetarian Foods. It took a bit of doing for Mother Ramona to convert the family, but eventually she did. The turning point was when Father Ralph bit into a Vitality veggie hot dog and said, "Well I declare! It tastes just like the real thing! Ramona, I always knew you were the queen of the kitchen, but now you're even better! You're a *Vitality Vegetarian Foods* Queen!"

This, of course, was Mom's cue to launch valiantly into "I'm a Vivacious VVF Cook." The song went surprisingly well. The words were on the monitor screens, and there was a sound track with singers to keep everybody straight. The tune was catchy enough so that by the time she got around to the chorus again and raised her rolling pin, the audience joined in with a roar, and applauded wildly when the skit was over.

*   *   *

"Justin, look!" Kirk said, holding the tiny screen on his digital camera in front of his friend's face. "Don't you want to see yourself?"

"No," Justin moaned.

The banquet was over. Darby and Mom had circulated among the tables for a while to greet the guests, but now the Case and Joylander families, along with Kirk, had gathered in the Case's suite.

"A great banquet," Donald Joylander said enthusiastically. "Cora was ecstatic. Especially since the merger talks went perfectly. Robert," he said, glancing at Dad, "isn't it time to answer some of my questions now?"

Mom and Darby were off to the side giggling about the skit. Mom turned her head to face them. "Questions about what?" she asked.

"Several things," he said. "The microphone in my office. And why the kids are mixed up in this."

Darby sighed. "I've got a confession to make," she said. "Papa, I'm sorry."

He cocked his head sideways. "Sorry? About what?"

"I made a CD I shouldn't have."

His jaw fell.

"It was just something I made as a joke because I was so frustrated about having to keep on doing the cute little Darby act."

He smiled wearily, and nodded. "We've exploited you a long time, sweetheart. Let's close the book on that, all right?"

She stared at him. "You mean I won't have to be Teenage Darby after all?"

"No, Darby, you won't. Let's finally give you a chance to be a normal girl. No matter what your Great-grandma Cora says, I'm sticking to that."

She put both palms on her cheeks. "Oh, Papa," she said numbly. "That's the best thing—" Suddenly her head went down and she burst into tears.

"Darby," he asked anxiously, "what's wrong?"

She sniffed. "The CD."

"Forget the CD," he said gently. "You said it was a joke."

"But I don't know where it is," she sobbed. "I don't know who has it. I don't know where it'll turn up. I said some really cruel things on it."

Robert Case joined the conversation. "She's right, Don," he said. "I'll tell you the whole story later, but someone has that CD and has been blackmailing your daughter with it."

"No they don't, Dad," Justin said.

Donald Joylander's mouth dropped open again. He glanced from Dad to Justin to his daughter.

"Sure they've got it," Dad said.

"No, Dad, the blackmailers do not have Darby's CD."

Dad frowned. "Justin, this is no time for one of your jokes."

"I'm not joking," Justin insisted. "The blackmailers heard Darby describing the CD on the microphone bug. And later they heard Darby and me talking about how she'd lost it. So they pretended they had it."

"How do you know all this?" Dad said.

Justin pulled out his black notebook. "It's all in here. I just did like you've always told me—observe things carefully and get them down on paper. Something they said was on the CD wasn't actually there."

"Justin," Darby said tensely, "if you're right, if they don't have the CD, then who does?"

"I do." The voice belonged to Tovah Case.

Dad's head whipped around. *"You've* got it, Tove?"

"I *think* I do," she said. "I just thought of it now. Remember the tour on Monday? We'd ridden that train all through the factory and finally got back to the Heritage Room. I got out of the little car I was riding in, and there almost at my feet was a CD in a case. It had your name on it, Darby."

Now it was Darby's turn to be open-mouthed.

"I'd forgotten all about it until now," Mom continued. "I think I slipped it into that big bag your dad gave us at the start of the tour, the one with all the veggie food samples in it. I guess it slithered way down to the bottom. I must have been so rattled at having to learn that song that the CD just vanished from my mind."

She got to her feet, went to a closet, and drew out the big brown bag. She felt around inside it. "Is this it?"

Kirk scrambled over to where she stood. He removed the CD from her fingers and popped the jewel case open. "This is it," he said.

"Give it here," Darby commanded.

"No," Kirk replied.

"Kirkie," she said in a deadly voice, getting to her feet, "you give me that CD now, or I'll—"

Instead, he held it between his two sets of fingers. He pushed upward with his two thumbs, and there was a clean little *snap*.

Darby gasped. Then she swallowed hard a couple of times and walked over to him. Taking the pieces from his hands, she snapped them into smaller and smaller and smaller pieces.

And then everybody clapped and hugged each other.

And Dad told the story of the mashed peas, with lots of gestures, and he ran a little bit too. And then they all sat down and turned on the local TV station.

* * *

"Justin," Robbie said much later as they were trying to get to sleep, "guess what."

Justin yawned. "What?"

"I heard Mr. Joylander talking with Dad before they left."

"Mmm."

"Dad's going to ask you a question tomorrow, and I know what it is."

Justin's eyes blinked open. "What is it?"

"You've gotta promise me one thing before I tell you."

"Promise what?"

"You've gotta cut down on the knock-knock jokes," Robbie said firmly.

"Why, what's the question?"

Robbie paused a long time, then said, "Mr. Joylander was really grateful to you for finding that hidden microphone."

"Dad found it."

"Yeah, but it sounded like you figured out that it was there in the first place."

"What's the question?" Justin asked again.

"Don't tell Dad I told you," Robbie growled.

"OK."

"Want to spend a week in Australia with me?"

Justin lunged upward, flung off the covers, and landed on the floor. "Yessss!" he shouted.

"Only if you choke off the knock-knocks."

"I'll try," Justin said.

"Oh, one other thing. Australia can be fun, but sometimes it can be dangerous."

As it turned out, Robbie was right on both counts.

When the Cases were eating breakfast the next morning, Kirk and Darby knocked on the door of Room 422 to say goodbye.

"We'll come back," Darby said hastily when she saw they were at the table.

"No, come on in," Mom said. "Have you two eaten yet?"

The two visitors shook their heads no.

"You haven't? I've got plenty left over—and I need to get rid of it before we leave." And before they knew it, Darby and Kirk were seated at the table with huge plates of fruit and toast and cereal in front of them.

"I feel bad eating all your food," Darby murmured between bites.

"No problem," Mom said. "Remember, I'm the Veggie Queen. You crowned me last night. I can handle it."

Kirk chuckled through a piece of toast. "OK, since you're the queen, maybe I can ask you a question. You believe in the Bible, right?"

Mom nodded.

"Then how come the Bible doesn't seem to say all that much about what to eat?" Kirk held up what was left of his toast. "I mean, it doesn't say to have a lot of fruit and toast and cereal for breakfast. It doesn't say"—and he shot a sideways glance at Darby—"to lay off the caffeine and the cheese curls."

Mom smiled. "Good question. The reason is that people

were already eating a lot of healthy food."

"I guess you're right," Kirk said. "The last couple of verses of Genesis 1 tells what God told Adam and Eve to eat."

"Exactly." Dad reached over on a side table for his Bible. (Fill in the blanks in the following verses, which are taken from Genesis 1:29, NIV): "Then God said, 'I give you every _____ - _____ _____ on the face of the whole earth and every _____ that has _____ with _____ in it. They will be yours for _____.' "

"See, Darb?" Kirk said, elbowing her. "Soybeans!"

Darby wrinkled her nose at him. "That sounds like a whole lot more than just soybeans," she said. "But Mr. Case, didn't God allow meat-eating later on?"

Dad nodded. "He did. But even then He made sure to list which animals we could eat and which ones we couldn't. You'll find that list in Leviticus 11. Check it out and you'll discover that most of the unclean animals are nature's garbage-disposal units. Their bodies can take in decayed flesh and even a bit of poison, and it doesn't bother them much. But if we eat their flesh, guess where the poison goes."

"And," Mom added, "Bible scholars and archaeologists know that the average person who lived back then didn't eat a lot of meat."

"Why not?" Darby asked.

"Because," Mom replied, "every time a farmer killed a cow or a sheep, it was one less animal to produce milk or wool—or to give birth to more cows and sheep. In Bible times, meat was eaten only on special occasions. There weren't any Billy's Bigger Burger restaurants. And these days, a lot of hormones and other things are pumped into cattle and other animals that weren't present in Bible times. So when you go down to Billy's, you're getting lots more than just meat."

"Of course, today we know much more about the benefits of a vegetarian diet," Mom stated. "That's why we don't eat meat."

"But why is this all such a big deal?" Darby asked. "I mean, when Jesus comes back, isn't He going to give us brand-new bodies? Why can't I just eat what I want until then?"

Kirk snapped his fingers. "There's a verse—I can't remember where it is—about the body being a . . . Somebody help me."

"I think I know the one you're talking about," Dad said, flipping to the last part of his Bible. "It's First Corinthians 3:16. 'Don't you know that you yourselves are _____ _____ and that God's _____ lives in you?' And over here in First Corinthians 10:31 it says, 'So whether you _____ or _____ or whatever you do, do it all for the _____ of God.'"

Kirk nodded. "Our minds live on top of our bodies," he said.

"Right," Mom said. "And if we're putting damaging things into our bodies, such as alcohol or drugs or too much fat or sugar, then our minds can't stay clear to really get to know our Creator the way He wants us to."

Kirk eyed what was left of the breakfast. "Well," he sighed, "if this is God's way of eating, I'm making it my way."

Tovah Case's Granola Recipe

8   cups rolled oats (or 4 cups rolled oats and 4 cups rolled five-grain cereal)

¾   cup pecan pieces

1   cup raw walnut pieces

1   cup raw, unsalted sunflower seeds

1   cup maple syrup

1   tsp. salt

2   Tbsp. vanilla

1   Tbsp. maple flavoring

1. Preheat oven to 250°F.
2. Mix all dry ingredients together in a large bowl.
3. Stir vanilla, maple flavoring, and maple syrup together in a small bowl, then add to dry ingredients and mix well.
4. Place granola evenly on two large nongreased cookie sheets.
5. Bake 1 hour and 15 minutes or until dry. Stir halfway through to keep granola from sticking to cookie sheets or burning.

You may substitute almonds for the walnuts or pecans, or add coconut to the dry mixture. After baking, you can add chopped dried fruit, such as apricots or raisins. For another option, add some fresh banana and apple slices on top of your granola before adding soy or rice milk.